The Whipping Boyfriend

EDWARD REED

Lu Ru
ENJOY!
5-14-16

authorHOUSE®

AuthorHouse™
1663 Liberty Drive
Bloomington, IN 47403
www.authorhouse.com
Phone: 1 (800) 839-8640

Published by AuthorHouse 02/03/2016

ISBN: 978-1-5049-7802-6 (sc)
ISBN: 978-1-5049-7801-9 (e)

Print information available on the last page.

Any people depicted in stock imagery provided by Thinkstock are models,
and such images are being used for illustrative purposes only.
Certain stock imagery © Thinkstock.

This book is printed on acid-free paper.

Because of the dynamic nature of the Internet, any web addresses or
links contained in this book may have changed since publication and
may no longer be valid. The views expressed in this work are solely those
of the author and do not necessarily reflect the views of the publisher,
and the publisher hereby disclaims any responsibility for them.

To Georgianna T. Collins

Chapter 1

He will be tall and from faraway, Dora thought and smiled. It was Tuesday and lately Tuesdays were becoming Dora's favorite day at the office. On Tuesdays she saw Chip.

Dora Ashworth had eyes for Chip Fowler. Something about him stirred her, and she was beginning to sense the feeling was mutual. Most of the sales reps who visited the busy office where she worked were women. As for the few men who came in, well, they just weren't Dora's type. There was something different about Chip. Something about his boyish good looks made Dora's heart beat faster when the two of them exchanged hellos. Until this new, sharp-dressed man caught her attention, Dora had forgotten that her heart could beat at all.

Since her divorce Dora had chatted and swapped messages with a few guys she had met online. She had even attended a handful of meet-and-greets when her kids were with their dad during the summer, but that was it. Two years without dating was "just crazy," according to her friends, and they never let her forget it.

"You haven't even hit your peak," her best friend, Yvonne, was constantly reminding Dora. "Take it from a cougar, you've got cougar written all over you." Yvonne was definitely a cougar. Blessed with the body of a college cheerleader—which, with the help of a little plastic surgery, she was managing to hang on to even as she was rapidly approaching forty—Yvonne had her pick of men. Dora didn't.

Dora didn't feel like a cougar and really wasn't sure she wanted to—and definitely not if it was going to land her in the same kind of relationships Yvonne was forever stumbling around in. Truthfully, the only cubs Dora had room for in her life were the five who called her mama.

Still, not wanting to be a cougar didn't keep her from wondering what a relationship might be like, a relationship with someone like this new salesman. Chip Fowler, the nice-smelling salesman, always made it a point to spend a little extra time talking with her when he was in the office.

"He's tall and has a beautiful smile and the sexiest eyes you've ever seen," Dora told Yvonne. Yvonne always insisted on knowing the juicy details of Dora's love life, even as nonexistent as it was.

"Sounds like he might be the one," Yvonne said, listening to Dora's description of her mystery man. It was hot outside, and the two were sunning by the pool at Yvonne's condo. The two of them spent time there when Yvonne was between boyfriends and Dora's kids were off somewhere with their dad and his new wife.

"Think so?" Dora asked. She peeled back her swimsuit to check her tan line and admire the six-pack beginning to take shape since she had joined the gym. Tired of being roly-poly girl, Dora had been faithful to her workouts. She also never missed a session because Dora liked Frank, her trainer. Frank was the only man who had touched her in two years, and even though he was just doing his job, it still felt good to be touched by a man.

"Yeppers," Yvonne said, using an expression she had picked up from her most recent ex-boyfriend, Miguel. Yvonne and Miguel had lasted about two weeks until she saw him on an episode of a reality law-enforcement show and found out that his name was really Leonard. It turned out that he still lived at home with his mom, and the Porsche he had been driving Yvonne around in belonged to his dad.

"Elmira said, 'He'll be tall and from far away,'" Yvonne reminded her.

"Yes. Elmira and all her hocus-pocus," Dora replied, somewhat dejected. "When you are barely five feet, everyone is tall, and that faraway thing is a little on the vague side, don't you think? Everyone in this town is from far away."

"Good point," Yvonne mused as she sipped her rapidly melting frozen drink. She was trying not to let on that she was flirting with the lifeguard who was beginning to notice her.

"How I let you talk me into Elmira's little voodoo act I'll never know. Fifty bucks for her to tell me something I could have figured out on my own," Dora added.

"Well, she was right about Jeff's new wife having a tattoo."

Dora's lips pursed as she shot Yvonne a friendly sneer. "What twentysomething isn't covered in tattoos these days?"

"Not all of them," Yvonne answered, defending Elmira.

"Again, fifty bucks for Elmira to work her so-called mojo," Dora said. "That experience rates right up there with you taking me to see those geriatric male strippers and putting me in the hot seat," Dora said with a chuckle, recalling their little trip to Elmira's earlier in the summer.

Chapter 2

Elmira Miller, Dora's septuagenarian neighbor who lived a few houses up the street, claimed to be part gypsy and hence part fortune-teller. However everyone who knew Elmira knew her olive gypsylike complexion was from her tan-in-a-can lotion. She had become addicted to the lotion when her dermatologist removed a few possibly malignant moles from her back and said no more round-the-clock tanning.

"If she's a gypsy, I'm a man," commented Megan Taylor. Megan was another member of Dora's circle of friends who had joined Dora and Yvonne on their little magical mystery tour to Elmira's house. The house had taken on a sinister look after the handyman—who hung around after her husband, Freddy, died—discovered Elmira had no money and moved on. The shrubs hadn't been trimmed in three Olympics and were overtaking the house, which hadn't seen a fresh coat of paint since Reagan was in office.

The inside of Elmira's house was equally sinister. A tribute to the sixties, the house was decorated in the Woodstock style, complete with an army of lava lamps, beaded doorways, and crushed black velvet posters. The crushed velvet and all those lava lamps, along with a few candles, gave everything a Halloween-like glow. The carpet of course was avocado shag.

Elmira had set up a table and chairs in her special room, which doubled as a sewing room when she wasn't telling fortunes. The table, covered with a purple satin sheet, held a crystal ball, a pack of tarot cards, and some really spooky-looking candles.

After Yvonne had collected fifty dollars from each of the fortune seekers, counted it twice, and deposited it in a golden treasure chest by the doorway, Elmira made her grand entrance. Having double-dipped herself in liquid tan, Elmira looked extra gypsy. Her hair was bundled in a red kerchief, and she wore a dress she had found on sale at a costume shop. The outfit was more than convincing to anyone who hadn't seen her watering her driveway or walking her dog in her bikini on a pretty regular basis. Dora wasn't among them, nor were any of the others who gathered that night, eyes rolling, in the shadows of the repurposed sewing room.

Dora was last in line to have her fortune told, and by that time most of the candles had pretty much melted. Just she and Yvonne remained. Megan's boyfriend had machine-gun texted her to come home, and she hurried out as soon as Elmira read her cards. Kelly, who rode with Megan, had already had her fortune read and left too. Shortly after that, the cards revealed Jackie Smith's husband had a new love interest. Jackie, a newlywed and the most recent addition to Dora and Yvonne's tribe, gathered her purse and left for home in tears.

Finally it was Dora's turn to let Elmira work her magic. Snuggling into the seat across the table from the fortune-teller, Dora struggled to keep a straight face.

"You are very sad," Elmira said to Dora in a most mysterious voice.

Dora listened, wondering if she actually was sad. Maybe so but she didn't feel sad. Then again she wasn't a gypsy, and she didn't have a crystal ball. She was just a mere mortal who was out fifty dollars. Fifty dollars was enough money to have her nails done twice or to pay for quite a few trips to the tanning bed. Elmira was right, Dora decided. She was sad, especially when she thought of her fifty dollars in Elmira's little gold treasure chest by the door.

Dora listened as Elmira rambled on about this and that before finally getting around to the topic of love and men.

"He will be tall and from far away," Elmira whispered with a hiss, studying each card Dora turned.

Dora, with a smile that became even more skeptical, turned a third and fourth card, showing them to Elmira.

"I see a terrible storm with lots of wind and rain, a storm followed by calm, and I see two doves," Elmira announced with a sound of triumph. She explained that doves symbolize purity and sometimes marriage.

"Hmmm," Dora said and paused. She could go along with the purity but as for marriage, not happening. Elmira and all the fortune-tellers in the world couldn't see that far into the future. The past ten years of her life with Jeff Ashworth and the hell he put her through with the cheating and the divorce had soured her on all things marriage.

"How about a few specifics?" Dora asked, not trying to hide her skepticism.

Elmira brought her index finger in front of her pursed lips. "Don't disturb the cards," she said, pausing before she blew out the candle. During the pause, Elmira did see Dora's future and it made her smile. She wanted to tell Dora what wonderful things she saw for her, but she couldn't. Dora wouldn't have believed them anyway. So instead, Elmira said with a contented sigh, "And you will be happy," before blowing out the rest of the candles. The smell of scented candle smoke hung in the air as Yvonne and Dora made their way down the stairs and out of Elmira's house by flashlight.

"See you tomorrow, Elmira," Dora said before pulling the door closed behind her.

Elmira didn't say anything. Sitting in the darkness with her vision of Dora's future, she only smiled.

Chapter 3

It was probably Dora's circle of friends—the crew, as they called themselves on girls' night out—who had steered her away from the wonderful world of dating and relationships. Dora's friends talked a good game, always telling her, "You need a man," and "You can't stay single forever." Dora knew better though. She knew she could do badly all by her lonesome, which is exactly what she told her friends when they started playing matchmaker. But that didn't stop them from trying.

Dora was the only one unattached in her circle of friends except for Yvonne, and Yvonne wasn't really single. She was trolling.

"Yvonne, you're stringing so many men along behind you that you look like one of those deep-sea fishing boats trolling in the Gulf Stream," she was forever being told. Living so close to Wilmington and the Carolina beaches, Dora and her crew had had their share of fishing and romance adventures. Yvonne had even caught the captain of one of the local charter boats for a little while. It turned out that the captain was too wild even for Yvonne's taste, and she cut the line with him before things got serious.

"Just waiting on a good catch, and then I'll reel him in," Yvonne shot back with one of her trademark winks as she pretended to crank a fishing reel.

"Are you sure it's not the catch of the day you plan on reeling in?" Dora teased with a wink of her own.

Megan added, "It's more like the catch of the hour."

Yvonne just shook her head, letting everyone know that they were welcome to help her with the men situation. "In life you can either cut bait or fish," she would always say, quoting the charter boat captain she had thrown back.

"Especially you, little Miss Pandora," Yvonne teased Dora. She knew that Dora was far from a Pandora, or at least the Pandoras she knew. Dora was pretty in a plain and simple way, which sometimes made Yvonne just a little jealous.

Occasionally Dora entertained the notion of a relationship, but most of the time she didn't, and that was partly because of what she saw her friends going through. When their love lives were good, they were very good, but most of the time one of them had her heart in an emotional blender and the blender was set to puree.

Dora had five other reasons that made her hesitant about getting involved with a man: Alex, Beverly, Dani, Curtis, and Emily.

Jeff, their father, had picked out all of their names except for her youngest. Jeff's girlfriend at the time, Dora found out later, had chosen Emily's name. That was the girlfriend before the divorce and before Stacey, her ex's new wife. Dora never was really sure whom to thank for Emily's name.

Dora had considered changing Emily's name after finding out Jeff hadn't come up with it on his own but finally decided the name fit her baby girl as well as any name she could think of. Besides, changing Emily's name would raise questions without answers. Emily was already doing pretty well in the question department on her own.

For the most part Dora only entertained the idea of having a man in her life after watching an occasional chick flick—a notion that usually passed by the time the credits rolled and reality set in. She was pretty sure there was no way her kids were ready for a man in her life, and she doubted there was a man in her time zone ready for them.

"No man is going to want to get seriously involved with a mother of five children. Especially not teenagers and especially not mine," Dora told Yvonne as they pushed their grocery carts up and down the narrow aisles of the supermarket. They shopped together every Thursday for Double Coupon Day.

"You may be surprised, and besides you have good children," Yvonne said, trying to sound encouraging as she picked out a bottle of wine from the store's rather limited selection.

Yvonne was right; Dora did have good children. They were respectful and well behaved, and any trouble they caused was pretty minor. Recently Dani got caught smoking, Alex carved his name in his bedroom door, Beverly backed over the neighbor's mailbox twice while teaching herself to drive without permission, Curtis had come home from day camp with a black eye from fighting, and Emily was sent out of the church nursery for informing the other children that there was no Santa Claus.

"But there isn't one," Emily insisted all the way home from church. "I was just trying to tell them Santa Claus is their mommy and daddy." Emily's giving the other kids the 411 on Santa Claus would have been all right if one of the younger children hadn't started crying. The crying undoubtedly led to him hyperventilating, and when Emily wouldn't let go of the topic, the little guy finally threw up. That was when Mrs. Mary, patron saint of nursery keepers, had had enough and sent Emily out of the nursery and back to her mom.

Maybe she would date when her kids were older, Dora told herself. Besides, she didn't really like what she had to choose from. She had been on a couple of dating sites long enough to figure out that pretty much the same bunch of desperate hopefuls were on every one. Those dating sites looked suspicious to her. All of them were filled with pictures of shirtless men sporting outdated haircuts and posing next to motorcycles, boats, and airplanes. Dora decided long before her free trial memberships ran out that looking for love online was pointless, a virtual wasteland of broken hearts.

Of course there was the handful of available men at her church. She could date one of them, but bless their hearts, they knew her and her children, and any of them being interested in her was pretty unlikely. Dora, who was not attracted to any of them, actually found comfort in their lack of interest.

There had been one man at church, named Chuck, she had found herself somewhat attracted to. The two of them had shared a pew a few times and talked awhile after Wednesday night services while her kids were finishing up arts and crafts. Then one Sunday morning a woman showed up with him, his wife no doubt. Dora would have sworn he hadn't been wearing a wedding ring until that day. She was sure of it. A few weeks later, after his somewhat suspicious-looking wife starting joining him for services, the two of them slipped out of the sanctuary early. Dora never saw Chuck or his wife again.

None of the men at work appealed to her either, not that she would date them anyway.

Maybe I'm just too picky, Dora decided. She had just read an article, "Ten Ways to Meet Your Match," in one of those magazines she picked up in the supermarket checkout line. She primarily bought those magazines for horoscopes and crossword puzzles, but sometimes they had pretty good articles.

This particular one suggested leaving your options open, but it never said just how open. According to the magazine, while she was playing it safe and possibly shutting out a serial killer or two, she was most likely shutting out a lot of really nice guys as well. "Take some chances," the article recommended, "and be spontaneous."

Spontaneous sounded nice, but Dora knew better. She had watched enough of those late-night, unsolved homicide shows not to buy into that line of reasoning. She didn't want to end up in the freezer of some man next door.

Dora had decided a long time ago that she was going to keep on being picky, if that's what it was called. Picky alive is better than picky dead in a freezer any day, she told herself.

"You might be surprised," Yvonne said, pointing to a man weighing some tomatoes at the end of the produce aisle.

Dora replied with a grin, "I don't do Bermuda shorts or hairy backs."

Yvonne licked her lips and winked at the man as he looked up, tomatoes in hand.

"You really shouldn't," Dora hissed. "Yvonne, you're sick."

Yvonne giggled, hurrying toward the checkout with Dora following and the man in the Bermuda shorts not far behind.

Once in Dora's minivan, the two of them caught their breaths. "Did we lose him?" Yvonne asked. She pulled on her floppy beach hat to disguise herself as she watched the man look around the parking lot.

"Yeppers," Dora replied, having picked up Miguel's word from Yvonne.

"Name one man you know who wants a ready-made family with five children," Dora said to Yvonne as she maneuvered the minivan through the busy parking lot.

"Remember the one in that movie we watched a few months back?" Yvonne said.

"My point exactly. That stuff only happens in the movies," Dora responded before asking Yvonne if she wanted a milk shake.

"I'm on a diet," Yvonne answered with a hint of pre-guilt.

"Me too," Dora said. She turned the minivan onto the highway and headed toward Mighty Burger, one of those burger stands famous for super thick shakes in three thousand flavors using real ice cream.

Chapter 4

Dora was just getting into her milk shake when her phone went crazy. Yvonne's shake was long gone, and she was eating some chili-cheese fries. "Forget the diet," she had said as she ate the fries with abandon. "Not bad," Dora said as she tried one, and that was when her phone went to DEFCON 2 or "blast" as Dani called it.

It was Emily.

"Mommy, when are you coming home?" she asked, sounding bossy, as if she had her hands on her hips.

"In a little while. Aunt Yvonne and I are shopping," Dora answered, taking another sip of her milk shake.

"Well, Daddy called and said you better get home right now, and he means it," piped Emily.

"Say that again, honey," Dora replied.

She set her phone to speaker so Yvonne could hear. Shaking her head, Yvonne just listened as Emily repeated her dad's message.

Dora assured Emily that she was on her way home as they spoke. She told Emily to pass that on to her dad if he called back.

"He's not calling back. He's on his way over," Emily added.

"Even better," Dora muttered. "Well, honey, ask him to cut the grass when he gets there."

Emily was quick to remind her mom that cutting the grass was Alex's job.

"Well, Alex needs some help," Dora said. "Just tell him. Daddy will understand."

Dora hung up and took another long sip of her cappuccino shake. This was the first time she had tried the flavor and she liked it, maybe a little too much.

"See what I go through with Jeff?" Dora said as the phone rang a second time.

It was Dani calling now. "Mom, guess where Dad and Granola Girl are on their way to?" she said, sounding more put off than usual. Her kids sometimes called their new stepmother Granola Girl, claiming that granola was all they ever saw her eat.

"Our house," Dora replied, thinking she would surprise Dani by already knowing.

"No, Mom. He's going scuba diving in Aruba, and he's taking her," Dani explained.

Dora tried to block images of her ex-husband drowning from her mind. She couldn't.

Somehow Dora was able to convince Dani that it was okay for her dad and his new child bride to go scuba diving and they would talk about it more when she got home. Dora was seriously considering getting Dani into counseling. The divorce had been hardest on her.

Her conversation with Dani had hardly ended, and Dora was just about to turn her attention to what remained of her shake, when her phone rang a third time. It was Alex. In a tirade of frustration, he spouted to his mom, "Dad's not paying for my baseball camp again this year, and he promised he would. Mom, he makes me so mad."

"Don't worry. We'll line up some yards to cut. We'll come up with the money," Dora said, trying to smooth things over.

"I know, Mom," said Alex, who used to think his dad hung the moon. "I just hate it when Dad does this junk to me. He's such a liar."

Dora listened, thinking to herself, *If Alex only knew what a liar his dad really is.* Sometimes she wanted to tell her kids everything; instead she just listened, frustrated for them.

After Alex said good-bye, Dora studied her phone, wondering if her other two children would be calling her. Hitting the bottom of her shake, Dora's straw made that familiar sound that lets you know there's no more good stuff. To her surprise, Curtis and Beverly didn't call.

"Cut your grass?" Yvonne asked with amused curiosity.

"Yes. That reminds good old jilting Jeff of something that happened when we first married. It's a long story," Dora said, lying just a little. The "cut the grass" thing was Dora's get-out-of-jail-free card that she played when Jeff got out of hand. The grass she was referring to was the marijuana crop Jeff had grown behind the bookshelf in his garage. Dora knew all about it. She knew because he had one just like it in their garage when they were married. Dora didn't play the grass card often, but she would if she had to. Jeff showing up at her house uninvited, especially with her not home, was a "have to" situation.

Not being satisfied with Dora's answer, Yvonne turned her focus to Dora's love life. "Anything new in the Chip department?" she asked, sniffing for clues about Dora's budding romance in her own little innocent way.

Dora shared that she and Chip had talked awhile when she was on her lunch break and he was setting up a presentation for the doctors.

"And?" Yvonne asked.

"We just talked," Dora said. "He's divorced, lives in Jacksonville, and has a daughter who stays with her mom in Virginia, and he plays on a church softball league."

"What kind of church?" Yvonne asked.

"Bapticostal," Dora answered.

"That's a new one on me," Yvonne replied, looking confused.

Dora was sure Yvonne would catch on to her joke, but when her friend didn't, she added, "I think he's a Christian who attends church on the big three."

"Big three?" Yvonne asked. Before Dora could explain, Yvonne had figured out that the big three boiled down to Christmas, Easter, and funerals. Yvonne fit into this group of believers too.

"I've got to get this thing looked at," Dora said, fiddling with the knobs and buttons of her minivan's air conditioner. It was scorching as the late afternoon sun began to bear down on Dora's minivan, and its air-conditioning felt more like a hair dryer. One of Dora's neighbor's had been promising to fix it for months.

"Anything else? Any phone calls or text messages?" Yvonne asked, pressing for more details.

"Nope," Dora said, lying again and beginning to feel her nose grow. Chip had asked her for her number, and she had given it to him.

"Why must I lie to my friends?" Dora asked herself aloud after Yvonne had disappeared in her convertible with grocery bags full of yogurt, wine, and massage oil.

She answered her own question with two words: social and media. It was Yvonne's second addiction; love was her first. Dora was sure that even before her groceries were put away, Yvonne would post pictures of their shopping trip on her Facebook page. Lately it seemed Yvonne's selfie stick was permanently attached to her hand.

Dora started her favorite part of shopping—
lugging the groceries across the yard, up the steps,
and into the house. Wondering where her kids were,
Dora almost called them to help but decided not to.

The Ashworth house was silent. Having scavenged
for supper, the kids were settled and settled was a
good thing. Dora noticed someone had left the lid
from the peanut butter jar sitting in the middle of
the counter.

"Ants are going to get in the peanut butter," Dora
hollered out so all could hear. There were no replies,
and Dora put the lid on the jar, wondering how ants
would taste in peanut butter. Lately she was always
wondering things like that. Maybe it was a sign.

Chapter 5

When a beautiful long-stem rose was delivered to Dora, it surprised everyone at the office. But the rose, with a card attached from someone named F. C. who had signed with a winking smiley, surprised Dora most of all. The doctors Dora worked for hardly noticed, but everyone else did.

Her coworkers were buzzing with puzzled curiosity. In twenty years Dora had never received flowers at work. They all wanted to know who F. C. was. Well, almost all. Greta Smith, the insurance claims lady who stayed at odds with everyone in the office, just shook her head each time she looked at the lonely little flower.

"Someone special you not telling us about?" Mary Anne asked, watching Dora blush.

"Just a friend from church," Dora said, "F for friend and C for church." This ended most of the guessing games as to who F. C. was, and Dora was glad. The guesses had been getting further and further off target. She really got a laugh at how desperate the guesses had become when someone suggested F.C. might be Frank Caldwell. Caldwell was the office's oldest patient. He was ninety-seven.

Dora was glad that the sender was either dyslexic or as private as she was and had reversed his initials.

Chip Fowler had sent the rose, but his name never came up. No one would have believed that the dream man everyone melted for would send a rose to her. Even if Chip had delivered the rose himself, she was pretty sure the entire office would have said "not." Dora didn't have a lot of confidence.

That afternoon she placed the rose in the drink holder below her minivan's struggling AC and sent Chip a text: "You shouldn't have." Chip sent her back a smile.

Studying his message, she was glad he hadn't replied with hugs or kisses. Dora wasn't up for hugs and kisses, and she really wasn't sure how comfortable she was with the rose, but it was pretty and the attention was nice.

In the mid-August heat, Dora felt herself wilting along with her rose, and she hoped the two of them would make it home before completely melting. They did.

Chapter 6

Having made it into the house without anyone noticing her rose, Dora set it on the kitchen counter between the microwave and the coffeemaker. It wouldn't attract a lot of attention there, and she could still look at it. The downstairs was quiet, too quiet. Nobody was lying on the sofa watching television or playing video games, which was a little unusual. The dishes were done and put away, and the living room had been picked up and vacuumed. When she had left that morning, the place looked like a train wreck, actually a couple of train wrecks.

"Hmm." Dora looked around. She was pretty sure something was up, and if she had noticed that the yard had been cut, she would have had no doubt.

The only two children home were Curtis and Emily. Alex was at baseball camp, Beverly was dog sitting, and Dani had called her earlier to ask if she could spend the night with the Baileys who lived in the neighborhood. They had a pool, and Dani and Alison Bailey were practicing for swim team tryouts.

"Come out, come out wherever you are," she said, trying to tease her kids from their hiding places. Curtis and Emily loved when their mom played hide-and-seek with them. They always hid in the same places: Emily in the broom closet and Curtis behind the couch. Checking the broom closet and finding it empty, Dora was puzzled until she heard someone scampering around upstairs.

"Curtis ... Emily ... come on down. You're the next contestant on the slice is right. Mama's got pizza," she hollered upstairs where she heard whispering voices. Pizza would bring them down; it always did. Especially Emily who hadn't caught on that sometimes Mom was tricking her.

Quietly down the stairs they came, one step at a time, which was out of character for Curtis. He was wearing a serious look on his freckled face, which was even more out of character for him, unless he had been fighting.

Emily was crying. Something was really up, and Dora was almost afraid to guess.

"Where's the pizza?" Curtis asked, looking around.

"I hope it's pepperoni," Emily added, wiping tears from her eyes.

It took a minute for the two of them to realize they had been had by the old pizza trick. Then Emily really started crying and wrapped her arms around Dora.

"What's wrong, kiddo?" Dora asked, trying to hide the fear of the unknown that had been steadily growing as she wondered what Curtis and Emily had broken, killed, or burned up.

Emily pointed toward the living room in the direction of the bay window, which had some panes shattered.

"How?" Dora asked. She listened as Curtis explained that he had been teaching Emily how to shoot a slingshot when they accidentally broke the window a couple of times.

Dora told Curtis that he didn't own a slingshot.

"Now I do," he announced, holding up a homemade version. He had made it from plans he found in a wilderness survival magazine.

"Three? It took three windows?" Dora asked, trying to hide her anger when she noticed Curtis tearing up.

"You guys, this house is all we have," Dora explained. She knew that what she was telling her kids wasn't totally accurate, which made her want to cry too. Her ex-husband and his attorney had finagled the divorce agreement so the house would eventually belong to him. Somehow she had managed to keep this to herself.

For now though what she was saying was true. It was their home. It was where Dora had grown up too. Her mom and dad had built the house when she was small and the neighborhood amounted to only a handful of homes. That wasn't the case any longer, and the house in which she had lived since she was Emily's age had plenty of company. Dora didn't mind though. She had nice neighbors, and it was a good place for her to raise her children. There was plenty of room and a big yard where her kids rarely spent any time, but it was there when they wanted to.

A two-story house with somewhat of a Tudor look, it had reminded Dora of a gingerbread house when she was a kid, and it still did on the rare occasions when it snowed. Her parents decided to downsize around the time Alex, her oldest, came along and had sold the house to her and Jeff as a wedding present. They had moved to Florida, leaving behind Dora's grandmother Mabel who had lived in the mother-in-law apartment over the garage.

Grandma Mabel had been a big help with Alex, Beverly, and Dani, but by the time Curtis was born, she was getting older and the steps up to the apartment were too many. Grandma Mabel moved to Florida too.

When she called, which she did pretty often, Grandma Mabel always asked how the flowers were and if the hibiscus was blooming. Not sure exactly which plant the hibiscus was, Dora always said yes. When she was growing up, Dora and her father had spent a lot of Saturdays planting shrubs and trees— live oaks and oleander—which after all these years worked together to create quite a scene. It was a scene that reminded Dora of her childhood and her father.

Dora's house had a fireplace, a double carport, and four bedrooms upstairs and two down. For years Jeff had talked about closing in the carport but never got around to it, and Dora was glad. The house had a wraparound porch and an extra large kitchen that Dora's mom had insisted on. Every window was sixteen over sixteen, and all of the door handles were glass.

Other than needing paint and new shingles and a few cracks in the sidewalk patched, the old house was in pretty good shape.

"You know what this means?" Dora asked, looking into the tear-filled eyes of her two youngest.

"We're grounded," Curtis answered.

"No pizza," added Emily.

"Nope," Dora said. She marched them into the living room where she made it very clear that the two of them would be paying for the window repair.

"Just like the antique shop, 'You break, you buy,'" Dora said in her sternest tone, which wasn't all that stern and didn't have to be as the two stood wondering what was going to happen next.

Sadly Emily turned her head down and admitted she had no money. Curtis said what little money he had wasn't enough to buy a pack of chewing gum.

"Oh, you'll have some money. Tomorrow is Saturday, and you two are going to get yourselves out and earn some," Dora said. She described how the two of them were going to be up early every Saturday doing odd jobs until they had enough money to repair the windows, even if it took the next Saturday and the Saturday after that.

"That's Daddy's weekend," Emily told her mom.

"Then the Saturday after that," Dora said. She always got a little put off about being reminded of Daddy's weekend, as the kids referred to the two days a month Jeff cooled his jets long enough to spend time with them.

Having figured out a short-term solution to the broken window, Dora sent Curtis to the garage for a cardboard box and Emily upstairs in search of tape. She rounded up a pair of scissors and a ruler from one of the kitchen drawers. In no time squares of cardboard replaced the broken panes of glass. "It's not pretty, but it'll do," Dora said, feeling somewhat satisfied.

"Now, let's go for some pizza," Dora announced, surprising Curtis and Emily who wasted no time heading for Minnie as they affectionately called Dora's minivan. Going out for pizza was a thrill for her children. Dora knew she was being easy on them, and they knew it too. She was being lenient because when she was around their age, she had broken the old bay window too. Only she had done it with a baton while practicing to be a majorette. Her father had been easy on her as well.

Backing out of the driveway, she studied the window and the cardboard panes. No one would notice, at least not for a while.

And so far no one had noticed the rose.

Chapter 7

The next day was Saturday, and around sundown Dora's other children made it home, gathering in the kitchen, hungry and irritable. Alex was always irritable after being away at baseball camp, and Beverly's dog sitting had turned out to be a disaster.

"I'm never doing that again," she exclaimed, looking around the kitchen for something to eat. She never bothered to explain to anyone what had gone wrong.

Dani, sunburned and exhausted from swimming all day, was irritable too.

Bummed out because the pizza from the night before was almost gone, Alex and Beverly each had a slice and headed to their rooms. Dani hung around the kitchen, wanting to be close to her mother.

"What's up?" Dora asked her sad-eyed, sunburned daughter.

"It's not fair not having a dad," Dani said as she connected the tiny, pepper-sized dots on the white Formica countertop. Visiting Alison, whose dad was a big part of her life, always left Dani a little down, and Dora knew it.

"Stop that," Dora warned her daughter. Dani put down her pencil and looked up, searching for some understanding in her mom's eyes, which she always found.

"I know," Dora said, but she really didn't. She had always had a father growing up, a good one. "I am not happy with it either," she added.

Dani licked the tip of her finger and was wiping away her artwork from the countertop when the door opened and Curtis walked in followed by Emily. They were tired but not too tired to beam triumphant smiles at their mom and sister. They had left that morning right after breakfast, and other than stopping in for some baloney sandwiches and grape drinks, they had been somewhere all day—working, they claimed.

When the two emptied their pockets onto the counter, there were far more bills than coins, which surprised Dora. She watched as they counted their earnings.

"Forty-one, forty-two," and with a sound finality, Curtis finished up with "forty-three."

Feeling left out of the counting, Emily laid two quarters on the counter, exclaiming, "And fifty cents," which Curtis echoed.

"Wow," Dora said, and she meant it. "That is incredible." And it was. She had expected them home before lunch complaining that they were hot, that they were tired, or that their legs hurt. Hurting legs had been Emily's recent excuse for getting out of chores.

"I think that should just about do it," Curtis said, trying to look and sound grown up.

"I believe it will," Dora said, smiling.

Sighing with relief, they told Dora about their day. They described in kid talk how they had helped Mr. Steve wash his car, and Blanche Anderson from around the corner scrub her sidewalk and repot some of her plants. Most of the money had come from Ms. Elmira, who kept them busy pruning her shrubs, edging her sidewalk, and giving her monkey grass a haircut.

"What's a gypsy?" Curtis asked. His lips were tight, revealing that his wheels had been turning on that question for a while.

"They're a kind of traveling people," Dora answered, wondering if her answer would satisfy Curtis.

"Ms. Elmira, she's a gypsy and she's not traveling," Curtis remarked.

"Who said she is a gypsy?" Dora asked.

"There was a car full of old ladies who stopped us on our way home and asked where the gypsy fortune-teller lived," Curtis shared with Dora.

"We told them we didn't know," Curtis said, explaining that the cars ended up turning into Ms. Elmira's driveway.

"And we watched through the bushes," Emily revealed. "It was two cars, and they were full of old women."

Dora shook her head when Emily mentioned them watching through the bushes. *More victims for Elmira*, Dora thought before shooing her two little spies upstairs for showers before supper. Dora had peanut butter and jelly sandwiches ready for them when they returned all clean and not smelling like monkey grass and work.

The Ashworth house went to bed early for a Saturday night, but everybody was tired. Dora sent Chip a text while she was working a crossword puzzle. He replied with a smile and a picture of a rose. Dora sent back a smile. Soon she and Chip were exchanging the details of their days. He told her how he had changed the oil in his new car and taken his daughter for ice cream and a movie. Chip's daughter, Amber, was thirteen, the same age as Dani. Dora tried to think of something interesting from her day to share with Chip. The only thing she could come up with was that she had her nails done. "What color?" he asked. Looking at her nails and feeling a little embarrassed, she typed in "Virgin Pink." Chip sent back a wink.

She was about to ask Chip about the movie he had seen with his daughter when Dani pushed open Dora's bedroom door and stretched out across the foot of the bed. She did this when she wanted to be close to her mom.

"Are you texting?" Dani asked, seemingly surprised that her mom would have a clue about how to send a text message.

"No, just setting the alarm," Dora said, feeling like such a liar.

"Ping" went her phone. It was another text from Chip. Dora wanted to check it but didn't.

"I'll set it for you," Dani volunteered, reaching for her mom's phone.

"That's okay, I got it," Dora said, pulling her phone close to her as she switched it off. Chip would have to wait. She could finish her conversation with him later when she had some privacy. He would understand.

"Let me brush your hair," Dora said, picking up a brush from her nightstand as Dani slid close to her. Soon Dani would be asleep. She always fell asleep when Dora brushed her hair.

"Pretty flower," Dani said, noticing Dora's rose as she began to drift off to sleep.

"Yes," Dora agreed. She had moved her rose from the kitchen counter to her dresser.

No more texts tonight, Dora decided, laying her silent phone by the lamp on her nightstand. Everyone was asleep and soon she would be too.

Chapter 8

"So, Mom, whose rose is that on your dresser?" Dani asked from out of nowhere on their way home from church Sunday. Dora wasn't as surprised by the question as she was by Dani taking so long to ask it. Then again Dani was like that; she processed things at a different speed. Dora referred to her as her slow cooker and supposed it was because Dani was guided by her heart rather than her head. Of all her children, Dani was most like Dora.

Dora was glad Dani was riding shotgun and that the windows were down. That way their little question-and-answer session wouldn't involve the others. Dora hated to lie to all five of her children at the same time, and especially on Sunday, but there was no way she was going to tell Dani where the rose came from.

"It was a gift from one of the pharmaceutical companies that has an account with the office," Dora replied. "It's pretty, isn't it?"

"Yes," Dani answered. "I was looking at it this morning."

"Oh yeah?" Dora asked, knowing better than to try to avoid Dani's questions. That would only make her more curious. Dora didn't mind satisfying Dani's curiosity, but this wasn't the right time to mention men or the possibility of her going on dates.

"I thought it might be from a man," Dani said, still not satisfied with her mom's answer.

"Actually the pharmaceutical rep who gave it to me, Chip Fowler, is a man," explained Dora.

"But not a man man?" Dani replied, asking and telling at the same time.

"Man man, what is a man man?" Dora asked, thinking that Chip was definitely a man man, but Dani didn't need to know that.

"You know the kind of man who wants to date you," her daughter went on.

"Would there be anything wrong with that?" Dora asked Dani, who was looking out the window.

"I guess not, if you two are just friends," Dani answered and changed the subject before her mom figured out how she really felt. Dani was too late; Dora already knew.

In the back of the minivan, the other kids were in their own worlds and hadn't picked up on Dani's question or her conversation with Dora.

Most likely Emily and Curtis would be okay with her dating, but Dora was anticipating lots of questions. As for Alex and Beverly, they were busy doing their own things. They probably wouldn't care one way or the other about her seeing someone. That was unless things got serious and whomever she was dating started hanging around and cutting in on their time and transportation. Dora couldn't have been more wrong.

Of all five of her children, Dani would have the hardest time with a new man in her mom's life. Even though Jeff turned out to be a disappointment in the dad department and was starting a new family, Dani still hadn't been able to let go. Dora was pretty sure that deep in her heart Dani wished her mom and dad could get back together.

"Who's going to cook me pancakes?" Dani asked a few weeks after Jeff had moved out, and that was only the beginning of such questions. She was sure that no one could ever make pancakes for her like her dad—pancakes with raisin eyes and a cherry for the nose, freckles of cinnamon, and a whipped cream smile. Somehow Dora had managed.

"As good as your dad's?" she asked Dani after serving up her version of a Jeff Ashworth pancake.

When Dani answered no, Dora decided it wasn't a fair question and she should have known what Dani would say.

"Won't go there again," she muttered to herself, feeling hurt.

At first, after Jeff had left her, Dora couldn't put the chain, which was forever coming off, back on Dani's bike, but after a while she learned. And she somehow managed to help Curtis with his math. Math had been Jeff's thing, and so was baseball. But since he left, Dora had learned all about fastballs, curves, sliders, and what it felt like to get hit with a wild pitch. She had been Alex's catcher many evenings before official baseball practice got underway.

Dora would be in denial if she said that she wouldn't like to have Jeff back, that is, if everything could have been the way it was before he started cheating. That was impossible though, and as hard as it was, this was the way things had turned out.

Turning onto her street, Dora's heart sank as she saw in the Sunday afternoon sunshine Yvonne's convertible parked in her driveway. Remembering that she and Yvonne had accepted an invitation to the beach wedding of one of their friends, Dora suddenly felt like throwing good old Minnie in reverse and letting Yvonne go by herself. The bride was more Yvonne's friend anyway.

"Might catch some flowers," Yvonne had teased Dora when she first mentioned the invitation. "Put you in the marrying mood."

"Doubt it," Dora said flatly.

The wedding wasn't until four, and with the beach not much more than an hour away, Dora figured why not. She would be back home by seven or eight at the latest, it would be nice to see the ocean and besides, Yvonne was doing the driving.

"No company," she told the kids who were busy in the kitchen making lunch.

"No company," they all replied in unison.

At the last minute Emily decided she wanted to tag along.

"Ask Aunt Yvonne," Dora told her. "It's her friend's wedding."

"Sure thing," Yvonne said. It would have been fine with her if all five of Dora's children piled in the back of her convertible, but she knew that wasn't going to happen.

Yvonne backed out of the driveway, her floppy hat flopping and her radio blasting, but that didn't matter to Dora and Emily who waved good-bye to Dani. Dani was sitting on the porch swing, eating a peanut butter and banana sandwich, and sketching the neighbor's cat.

The wedding was nice, and neither Dora nor Yvonne caught the bouquet. Some little old lady did. She held it up high and waved it as if it were the Olympic torch, a beacon for would-be suitors in the crowd. When no suitors appeared, the bouquet ended up in the old woman's seat. Dora saw it there on her way out of the church.

She remembered catching her sister's bouquet, and six months later she had one of her own to throw. Try as she might though, she couldn't remember who caught it. She had been too in love to remember much of anything about that day. The most magically wonderful day of her life, and it was all a blur and videotapes. The tapes were long gone even though the blur lingered.

Yvonne pulled into a Dairy Queen on their way home. "Weddings make me hungry," she said with a guilty grin.

"Me too," Emily said from the backseat with a grin of her own.

Chapter 9

A few weekends later, on Jeff's weekend, the kids were gone and Dora was home alone. Jeff and Stacey had picked up the children early on Friday afternoon before Dora got home from work. Finally they were off on a big weekend adventure: Friday, a camping trip; Saturday, an amusement park; and Sunday, a picnic. *How nice,* Dora thought as she had listened to her children's excitement grow after their father revealed his plan. They all had their things packed, even Dani, three days ahead of time and sat by the living room door waiting for Friday to arrive. Looking at the mountain of bags, Dora wasn't sure how Jeff was going to fit it all and the kids in his Land Rover. She decided that was his problem. Undoubtedly he had managed somehow. When she got home, the mountain of luggage was gone and so were her kids.

At first Dora didn't feel alone, but she knew it wouldn't take long. "Me time," she heard herself say, and for some reason the sound of "me time" lost its appeal. Yvonne was busy with her newest conquest,

Harold, who to everyone's surprise was ten years older rather than ten years younger than her. Dora had sent a text to another friend, Barbara, in hopes that the two of them could do something together. Not getting a reply, Dora gave up on the idea of that happening.

She decided it would be a pizza and movie night as she went upstairs to get out of her uniform, into the shower, and then into something comfortable.

Dora was just about to replay her favorite scene from *Grease*, where Danny and Sandy sing "You're the One That I Want," when her phone pinged. *Yvonne probably*, Dora thought, but she checked anyway. She was glad she did. It was a second text message from Chip. She somehow had missed the first one.

"What are you doing?" the second message said. It was followed by a smile.

"Having pizza and watching a movie," she texted back, wondering if she should mention that her kids were gone for the weekend. Maybe not, she decided.

"What are you doing?" she sent back.

"Watching some rerun on the History Channel" was Chip's reply. That must have been his way of letting her know he was home alone, she assumed.

At least an hour passed with their back-and-forth texting before it ended with Chip saying, "See you tomorrow at four o'clock. Can't wait."

Dora replied with a smile and then switched off the television and the lamp by the sofa, checked the front door, and headed upstairs to her room.

Once in bed, snuggling under her favorite comforter, she called Maria. Maria was her childhood friend. Growing up the two had been closer than sisters. Now they lived on opposite sides of the country. Maria would be excited to hear that Dora was finally going on a real date.

"You're going to have to do it sooner or later unless you plan on ending up like your aunt Gladys," Maria said with some foreboding. After divorcing, Aunt Gladys had sworn off men for good. Even after her children were grown and gone, Aunt Gladys was true to her word and never dated.

"Aunt Gladys never seemed unhappy," Dora countered.

"And she never seemed happy either, now did she?" Maria fired back. Dora could always count on Maria for being up front, and she knew what Maria said was true. Dora didn't want to end up like Aunt Gladys and definitely not because of Jeffrey Allen Ashworth.

Restless after hanging up with Maria, Dora lay in bed thinking about what she had in her closet. Not being able to decide between a sundress with sandals and her white capris with tennis shoes, Dora felt herself overcomplicating what should be simple and easy: picking out something to wear. Overcomplicating things came naturally to Dora. Chip had mentioned a walk on the beach and listening to the band, so her final decision was to wear the shorts she had bought on a recent shopping adventure with Yvonne, a T-shirt, and flip flops.

Gizmo, Emily's Chihuahua, had followed Dora up the stairs and onto the bed, and after listening to all of the girl talk was fast asleep long before she was.

Chapter 10

Four o'clock and the Surf City pier had seemed far off when Dora woke up that morning with a phone hangover from talking to Maria until her ear hurt, but Dora's day went fast. She was able to get through her Saturday routine of laundry and shopping with time left over for doing her nails and responding to a dozen or so text messages from her kids. All of the messages included pictures in which everyone was smiling. No matter how much they were whining in their messages about the heat and the bugs and how hard the ground was, Dora knew they were having fun. Her kids having fun and spending time with their dad meant a lot to Dora, even if she wasn't in their pictures anymore—and even if it meant there was another woman there instead of her. As long as her kids were happy, Dora was happy, though sometimes it was a sad kind of happy.

From the looks of things, everyone was going to come home in hiking boots. Jeff had bought boots for all five children, who were showing them off in every picture. When he wanted their shoe sizes, Jeff didn't say what he needed them for and she didn't ask. It was better between them or at least for her when they kept to the script.

The pictures of her children showing off their hiking boots were better than the ones from their big beach adventure in the spring. The photos the children sent her from their beach adventure featured Beverly in a skimpy bikini and Alex with tattoos all over his body. Fortunately the tattoos were the wash-off kind, and as for the Beverly's bikini, Dora had nipped that in the bud the next time she did the laundry.

"It just disappeared," Dora answered when Beverly started looking for her new swimsuit. "Just disappeared," Dora repeated, failing to add that she had helped the little swimsuit find its way into the bottom of the clothes hamper—the very bottom, where no one ever looked. "It'll turn up," Dora assured her all the while thinking, *Not on my watch*.

"I hope so," Beverly said, letting her mom know that Stacey, her stepmom, would be upset if it didn't.

"She will?" Dora asked a little irked.

"Yep, she picked it out for me. It's almost like hers," Beverly explained. The swimsuit was a lot like Stacey's but not quite. Stacey wore full-on butt floss.

At one point, when Stacey's name came up between her and Jeff, Dora almost told him that if he wanted another daughter, it would have been easier to adopt. But she didn't. She already knew his reply, and she didn't want to go there again, ever.

All of that was behind her now, and Dora was starting to regain a little of her confidence. She wasn't giving Stacey or Jeff any of her joy, even though one or both of them showed up in every picture her kids sent. Early on after the divorce, Dora did a lot of sitting and sulking, but in the past few months she had felt like she was coming out of her shell.

Looking at her watch and realizing she might be a few minutes late, Dora hoped Chip would understand. Maybe it's him, she hoped when her phone buzzed, but it was Yvonne.

"Harold asked me to invite you over," Yvonne said, "that is, if you aren't doing anything."

Yvonne went on to paint an invitation for Dora: a swimming pool, steaks on the grill, smooth jazz, and bottles and bottles of whatever she had a taste for. Yvonne had a way of making everything sound good, especially after a few glasses of wine. She was usually toasted when she sold most of her houses.

"And he's got a friend who wants to meet you," Yvonne added, as if meeting one of Harold's friends would be a bonus.

"Really?" Dora asked, trying to sound half-interested for Yvonne's sake.

"Yes indeed. Actually he's Harold's neighbor. He's a retired mailman," Yvonne answered, having dropped Miguel's "yeppers" for Harold's "yes indeed."

An image of her own mailman, Harvey Walker, flashed through Dora's mind. *That's just sick*, she thought. In his day Harvey had probably been beefcake, but it wasn't his day anymore. The notion of swimming around in a pool with him, Harold, or Harold's mailman friend made it easy for her to tell Yvonne she was busy.

"Suit yourself, home girl," Yvonne answered a little put off. "Just keep wasting your Saturday nights on crossword puzzles. That'll be just fine with me." Then she hung up. Yvonne got irritable when she was drinking, even just a little.

A few minutes later, Yvonne, who was feeling remorseful for being snippety with Dora, did what she always did after hanging up without saying good-bye. She called back. "If you change your mind, let me know," she said with a hint of an apology.

"I will," Dora said with an understanding voice. She was navigating her minivan across the four lanes of traffic and down the exit ramp, which she almost missed. *Surf City, here I come*, she thought as she peeled off of Highway 17 North while turning up the radio.

Quite a coincidence, Surf City beach twice in a month, Dora realized as she recalled the sign advertising plastic surgery complete with a scantily clad swimsuit model. The sign was next to the Dairy Queen where Yvonne had treated her and Emily to their after-wedding fix. It wouldn't take but a minute, so Dora talked herself into a quick bathroom break before meeting up with Chip and turned Minnie into the busy DQ parking lot.

"Are we still on?" Chip messaged her with a question mark.

"Yes, I will be there in five minutes," she sent back. At first she hadn't liked texting, but now that she was used to it, it wasn't so bad. What Dora liked best about texting was the way she didn't have to tip her hand and let Chip know how excited she was to see him. Dora's voice always gave her away.

The night before, the texting had come in handy. She was sure she would have gotten ahead of herself, especially if the two of them had been talking as they were thinking up something fun they could do together.

"Bowling?" he asked.

"Too noisy," she answered truthfully.

"A movie?" she offered to which he suggested something outside.

"How about beach music and a walk in the sand?"

She sent him back a smile. Now, with her hair in a ponytail and wearing a pair of Alex's cool sunglasses she borrowed off of his dresser, Dora strolled toward the pier where Chip said he would be waiting. Sitting at a picnic table, Chip was wearing shorts and a ball cap with some cool-looking shades too. He didn't look like the button-down and tie man she was used to seeing.

Raising his shades to get a better look at her as she walked up to the table, it was obvious she didn't look like the little all-business lady he was used to either. "You look great" was the first thing Chip said.

Dora wanted to say the same thing to him but caught herself and replied with a smile that said thank you. She was beginning to feel a cool breeze off the ocean.

"The band sounds good," she said, recognizing "Margaritaville."

"They play here every other Saturday," Chip said. Finishing his water, he took Dora's hand, and on their way to the bandstand, the two of them detoured to what looked like a little hut where they found some shade and a table. Leaving her alone for just a second, Chip returned with two bottles of ice-cold beer and a basket of what he introduced as "deep-fried sin."

Chapter 11

Heading toward home, Dora was still smiling from her date with Chip. In the gentle breeze with the ocean waves dancing, the two of them had spent most of the evening walking along the beach holding hands. The atmosphere had been incredibly perfect.

"I hope you had a good time," Chip said as they returned from their long sunset walk and made their way through the sand toward the lighted parking lot. With her flip-flops in one hand and Chip's hand in the other, Dora enjoyed the feel of the warm sand under her feet. Still caught up in the moment, she wasn't sure how to answer.

"I had a great time," she finally said, catching Chip's smile out of the corner of her eyes.

Dora did have a great time and in some ways wished that it could have lasted longer, but it couldn't. The drive home and the almost empty parking lot made that all too clear.

"See you next week," Chip said, standing beside Dora's minivan as the two of them talked through her open window.

"Tuesday," Dora said. She had already checked the calendar at work to find out the next time Chip would be in the office.

"Tuesday," Chip said, leaning into Dora's window to give her a quick kiss on her cheek. She loved the smell of his cologne. Dora turned slightly, drawing his lips to hers. It was a soft kiss and over before it started. They both smiled.

Maybe a kiss was too much for a first date. Dora finally decided probably not. Chip was definitely a kisser and affectionate, something Jeff hadn't been. She wondered why she kept comparing Chip to Jeff. She had caught herself doing that throughout the evening, and it was starting to bug her. It especially bugged her when it caused her to entertain the idea that she wasn't over Jeff.

Maria had been so right. Jeff had been the only man Dora had ever known besides the few guys she dated in high school, and Maria had warned her not to go looking for his replacement.

"You've changed, and if you go looking for another Jeff, you will only end up getting hurt," Maria explained. "Don't use Jeff as a measuring stick to compare other men to. Let him go. Not because he hurt you and did you wrong, but because letting him go is what's best for you. You've moved on."

Dora considered what Maria had said, retracing the time she had spent with Chip. He seemed like a really nice guy, and Dora could see herself falling for him, which scared her for a lot of reasons.

Chapter 12

Gizmo greeted Dora as she walked in the door, letting her know he was overdue for his nightly walk. Dropping her things on the bar, she snapped on his leash, and he led her outside into the shadows cast by the live oaks that lined the sidewalk. The moon was full.

It truly had been a nice evening. Dora trailed along behind Gizmo who, sniffing here and there, pattered as far from home as she would let him. Sitting on the bench in the neighborhood gazebo, Dora checked her phone. It had been on vibrate most of the evening until Yvonne had started blowing it up, first with calls and then text messages, forcing Dora to put it on silent. She knew her phone was loaded with so many messages and voice mails that she almost hated to look.

There was a "Hey, Mom" message and two pictures from Dani. One was of the kids on a roller coaster with their hands raised. In the second photo, everyone was sitting around a picnic table happily eating hot dogs. Dora missed them.

After Dani's message, Dora read Yvonne's, which ranged from "What are you doing?" to "Don't make me get out of this pool and come hunt you down and drag your butt over here."

Then there was a message from Maria, who wanted to know how the date had gone. Dora replied, "Wonderful."

Finally there was message from Chip. "Home safe?"

Smiling, Dora answered, "Yes and thanks." Not knowing what else to say, she almost hoped he would not reply. He didn't.

Taking his place at her feet after he did whatever it was he had to do, Gizmo looked up with eyes that let Dora know he was hungry. She ended up carrying him home after he saw a cat and got excited. It was after midnight, and she didn't want his barking to wake up the neighborhood.

Passing Elmira's house, Dora noticed several cars parked in her driveway. The glow of a bluish light in the upstairs window and the full moon explained everything. Elmira was working her magic again.

After their kiss in the parking lot and the wonderful time she'd had with Chip, Dora was beginning to think there might be something to Elmira's hocus-pocus routine after all.

Chapter 13

Before Dora could turn around, the weekend had vanished. Still excited from the adventure with their dad, the kids had rolled in late Sunday evening. They were sunburned and tired but not too tired to tell Dora about spending the night in the woods and to show off their hiking boots.

"Can you take us rock climbing, Mom?" Emily asked. She plopped down on the porch swing beside her mom, waiting to be rubbed down with aloe.

"Rock climbing?" Dora asked, fishing around for Emily to tell her more.

"Yes, Stacey does it and she's good at it, Mom," Emily explained. She gave a six-year-old's version of watching Stacey climb the side of some huge mountain way up in the sky. Stacey was undoubtedly part spider from the sound of Emily's story.

"How about a little tree climbing?" Dora suggested with a wink.

"Not without the proper equipment," Emily responded. She had a look of relief as Dora rubbed the cool aloe gel she had just taken from the freezer on the sunburned skin of Emily and Curtis.

Curtis, who had been quieter than usual waiting for his turn to get some sunburn relief, asked his mom about her date.

"Date?" Dora was caught off guard.

"Dad said we couldn't call you, that you were on a date," Curtis shared as he pulled off his T-shirt. His shoulders were blistered.

Feeling like she was on the outside looking in, Dora wondered how Jeff had known about her date and what the kids knew. Dora played possum. Little by little, as she worked the aloe into his sunburn, Curtis explained how Uncle Larry, Jeff's older brother, told his dad at the picnic that he had seen her and a man walking on the beach at Surf City. Dora had forgotten that Larry had moved to Surf City after he and his wife split up.

"I was down there listening to the band and ran into a guy, a salesman from the office. But it was hardly a date," Dora told Curtis, who didn't seemed convinced. "Besides, that was yesterday. What does that have to do with you calling me today?" she added, trying not to let her anger show.

"Dad said you were probably busy, and you needed some space," said Curtis, sounding a little confused as he leaned his head forward so Dora would keep rubbing his sunburned shoulders.

"All done," she said, putting the lid on the bottle of aloe and pulling Curtis onto her lap. Struggling to get up, he giggled while she kissed him and tickled him and held him closer than she had in a while. It was the only way she knew to answer the question that was troubling him.

Jeff's bother Larry was an all right guy, and Dora couldn't imagine him playing spy for Jeff. He just wasn't like that. Jeff had probably taken a harmless comment and, doing exactly what he was good at, had twisted it just a little. Whatever the case Dora didn't like it.

"How long did you stay?" Curtis asked.

"Where?" asked Dora, still trying to figure things out.

"At the beach, Mom," Curtis answered.

"Until dark. Why?" asked Dora.

"Just wondered," Curtis replied. He pulled on his T-shirt and plopped down on the other side of his mom. Emily had fallen asleep, her new hiking boots dangling from the swing. Soon Curtis would be asleep too.

None of the others mentioned their dad's comment about giving their mom space and her being on a date. Most likely they had found it unbelievable that she would even be on a date. Jeff's announcement undoubtedly had gone over their heads. Other than Curtis and his questions, it had been an open-and-shut case. Dani's questions about the rose and Curtis's query about her date were enough to let Dora know her kids might not be ready for her to introduce a man into their lives.

"They'll adjust," Maria had told her during one of their long talks. Dora wasn't so sure. She wondered how she would introduce Chip to her children if things between them ever got that far. Whether she was willing to admit it or not, part of Dora was beginning to hope they would.

"This is Chip," she imagined saying as she led him into the living room where the children would be watching television. Somehow that didn't seem right. Maybe it would be better if she made the introductions one at the time. Five children at once might overwhelm a mild-mannered father of one. Not sure how the children would accept her dating Chip, Dora tried to figure out which one would take it best. She already knew who was going to have a problem with it: her little sunburned snorer who was snuggled up against her in the swing.

Beverly had recently been scoping out men at church for her, and Alex had mentioned that his baseball coach was single. "You know, Mr. Jones is always hugging on you," Beverly told her over and over every Sunday on their way out of church.

"Mr. Jones hugs everybody," Dora said, fending off Beverly's suggestions.

"Not the way he hugs you," Beverly teased her mom.

Dora knew what Beverly said was true. But there was something about Mr. Jones that just didn't feel right to Dora, especially after she had seen him and Louise Frink, the choir director, come out of the cloak room all red faced before choir rehearsal one Sunday afternoon. As for Alex's coach, he was single because he wanted to be, and dating him would definitely qualify her as a cougar.

Maybe Aunt Gladys had it right all along, Dora decided as she sat on the swing between her two sleeping children. Yvonne had texted her earlier that afternoon to see what she was doing. Besides her texts, there had been no others. Not even a smile from Chip. Dora was beginning to second-guess their date and especially the kiss.

Thinking that Chip might be busy, she decided not to text him, at least not until later when the kids were in bed. Maybe then she would send him a smile if he didn't message her first.

Chapter 14

"A whipping boyfriend?" Dora asked.

"Yes," Maria answered.

"Sounds a little bit kinky," Dora replied with a suspicious chuckle. She wondered where Maria was going with this conversation. It sounded to Dora like something that could get you in trouble with social services.

Maria, putting on her professor's hat, explained how in the days of old, it was not allowed to punish children of royalty. "Instead they had stand-in children who took their whippings."

An image of Thomas Gainsborough's *Blue Boy*, which had hung in her aunt Gladys's living room, flashed through Dora's mind. There had always been something about the smug look on the boy's cherubic face that Dora didn't like. Listening to Maria, she was beginning to understand what it was. While the Blue Boy was strolling around the estate in his crushed velvet outfit, breaking windows and waiting for

Gainsborough to paint him, some poor kid was out behind the wood shed taking his whippings for him.

"That's just wrong," Dora replied, still not sure where Maria was going with this conversation.

"What you need, Dora, is a pre-boyfriend to warm your kids up to the idea of you dating—a whipping boyfriend, just in case they decide to rough him up. Someone you won't mind losing. Then after he's gone and you've established some boundaries, you can introduce this Chip guy. It's sort of a way to reach a compromise without the children being the wiser."

"Hmm," Dora responded, thinking out loud. "That doesn't sound very nice."

"I suppose you're right. It wouldn't be very nice if your whipping boyfriend isn't in the know," Maria agreed. "I guess maybe you could tell him up front. That way there wouldn't be any hurt feelings when the kids send him packing."

"You've done this?" Dora asked.

"Yes, actually by accident," Maria explained. "About a year after Kevin and I split up, I became interested in Robert, but he always seemed busy so I started talking to a guy named Cliff. It was just talk at first, but then we started going out. He wasn't really my type and he liked me more than I liked him, but that was okay. I enjoyed the attention."

"So, in other words, you used him," Dora interjected.

There was a pause. "I guess you could say that," Maria responded before picking up the story where she left off. "After a while I couldn't keep Cliff a secret. Kelly, my nosey one, kept up with every move I made. My girls were thirteen and fifteen then, and they were both going on twenty five."

"You brought him home?" Dora asked.

"No, not at first, but I wished I had. I took him to one of their basketball games instead. Kelly was playing, and Monica was on the cheer squad. It was a bad idea."

"What happened?" Dora asked, being drawn into Maria's story.

"Nothing really extreme, they just didn't speak to me for about a week," Maria said with a laugh.

"So how did it work out?" Dora asked. "You ended up marrying Robert."

"The girls didn't like Cliff at all, and they didn't hide it," Maria continued.

Dora imagined the attitudes of Kelly and Monica. She had babysat the girls for Maria a number of times before Maria and Kevin moved away. They were a handful as preschoolers, so she could only imagine what they had been like as teens.

"They gave poor Clifford a fit," Maria went on. "He couldn't do anything right."

"How long did it last?" Dora asked.

"I can't remember, but I know it was through Christmas because Cliff bought the girls bicycles." Maria paused to think back.

"So he liked the girls?" asked Dora.

"Yes he did, and that is the sad part. They weren't ever terribly vicious toward him; they just didn't accept him. Finally our relationship ended, and he stopped coming over," Maria concluded.

"Just like that?" Dora asked.

"Just like that, and everybody was glad. Even my parents were relieved."

"Robert stepped right in?" Dora asked.

"It was a good while before Robert and I started talking, but when we did things went pretty smoothly. Ten years later we're still happy," Maria said with a contented sigh.

"So how about Cliff?" Dora wondered, feeling a little sad at what seemed like a pretty nice guy getting hurt.

"Oh, it worked out for him," Maria said. "He ended up marrying the librarian at his school. I still see him around town."

Dora felt a little better hearing that it worked out okay for everyone. She was already wondering about a whipping boyfriend of her own. No one came to mind.

"So has anybody else used your strategy?" Dora asked

Maria named a few of her friends who had similar "first boyfriend after divorce experiences." Some were accidental and some were intentional.

"Survey says ... your children are going to have a problem with this Chip guy, and this is especially true if you're really serious about him. From the sound of it you are, whether you admit it or not," Maria added bluntly.

Feeling found out for having revealed how much she was attracted to Chip, Dora couldn't deny that Maria was right. After telling her that Curtis and Dani seemed suspiciously protective over her, she knew Maria was giving her good advice about making Chip her "first after the divorce" boyfriend. It wasn't going to work out too well.

They talked for a while longer before finally looking at their clocks and realizing how late it was getting, especially for Dora. Up past midnight for the third night in a row was taking a toll on her. She turned out her lamp and lay in the dark thinking about Maria's suggestions. A whipping boyfriend Dora decided just might not be a bad idea.

Three days later she found one.

Chapter 15

There was a long silence, and Dora strained to hear Maria's response, which finally came. It was Wednesday night, and Dora had called Maria with good news, but from the sound of Maria's sigh, it wasn't all that good.

"So you just picked up some homeless guy, introduced him to your children as your friend, and brought him home to stay in Grandma Mabel's bungalow," Maria said, summarizing what Dora had just told her. Maria was extra careful not to leave anything out.

"That's about it," Dora answered. She was almost sorry she had mentioned the whole thing, and even sorrier that it had happened at all. Maria was right to be concerned; she had been pretty thoughtless.

"So you just had a feeling about him, a complete stranger who happens to be a vagrant," Maria added.

"He looked like a good fit for a whipping boyfriend," Dora said, scrambling somewhat to defend her obviously not-so-good decision.

"Not exactly, sounds like the ingredients for one of those ax murderer movies. Please tell me your doors are locked and your kids are safe in the house," Maria said, and she wasn't smiling. Dora could tell.

"Yes, and the alarm is on too," Dora said smartly, hoping to cushion what was now looking like a pretty stupid mistake, not only to Maria but to herself as well.

"He looked like a good fit," Maria echoed Dora's earlier comment.

"Yes," Dora replied. She peeked through her bedroom blinds and out into the backyard. There was a light on in the apartment over the garage. "He must still be up," Dora mused about the man she had so recklessly moved into her life.

Dora had seen him that morning while waiting for the light to change. He had been standing by the bridge she passed under on her way to work, and he was holding a cardboard sign. Instead of the all-too-familiar sign that said, Will Work for Food, this man's sign said, It's Hard to Smile When You Are Hungry. The man had used a magic marker to print the bold letters on the tattered piece of cardboard. It touched something in Dora as she watched him standing in the pouring rain.

"Dora that was foolish. You don't know this man. He has to go," Maria said, her concern growing.

"How can I make him go?" Dora asked after inviting him to stay in the apartment that used to be her grandmother's.

"Those people are like stray cats. By tomorrow you may have a few of his friends hanging out around your house," Maria warned.

"He doesn't seem like the type," Dora said, still peeking out the window.

"They never do," Maria fired back, sounding a little strained.

"He's different," Dora whispered. The man she had invited home was different. How he was different she couldn't say, but there was something about him very unlike the bums she usually saw holding cardboard signs by the bridges.

"A bum is a bum, I'm telling you," Maria said emphatically. "I guess you cooked him supper too," she added with somewhat of a laugh. Dora could feel Maria lightening up a little, even though she was two thousand miles away and they were connected by telephone.

"So did he jump right in?" Maria asked, hungry for more details. Dora could feel her looking for clues.

"Not exactly," Dora answered. She remembered a look of hopeful confusion in the man's eyes when, on her way home from work, she had made a second trip around the cloverleaf and pulled up next to him. He had been standing there all day. The rain had stopped earlier and the sun was bright, but he was still soaked. Surprised suspicion would better describe what was in the man's eyes, and up close she realized he couldn't be much older than her.

"Actually I did buy him some chicken bites from the Mighty Burger," Dora explained as she unraveled the events that led up to the man staying the night in her grandmother's apartment. As the soggy man ate his chicken, Dora had explained to him that she needed a whipping boyfriend to get her kids used to the idea of her having a man in her life.

"So, in other words, you want me to lean into the strike zone and take one for the team," said the man sitting beside her. Finishing off his twentieth chicken bite, he wiped the honey-mustard dipping sauce from his beard with the back of his coat sleeve.

"I guess you could say it that way," Dora remembered saying. Now she wished she could backpedal, but for some mysterious reason she couldn't.

"How much are you paying him?" Maria got around to asking.

"Room and board," Dora answered, "until he can get back on his feet."

"On his feet," Maria said with a cackle. "You can't be for real."

"Yes," Dora said, sounding even sadder and more confused as the possible consequences of her thoughtless decision was starting to send up a cloud of red flags.

"The lights in the apartment are off now. He must be asleep," Dora whispered to Maria for some strange reason.

"Good," Maria said, sounding a bit less anxious. "It'll probably work out." Shifting the subject a little, she asked what the kids had to say.

"They're pretty confused," Dora answered, sounding a little confused herself. She recalled Beverly and Alex's reactions when she picked them up after band practice with a strange-looking man in the front passenger seat.

"Who's he?" Alex half-demanded. Dora could tell he was a little put off by the unsightly stranger. *Thank goodness we got rid of the cardboard sign,* Dora thought. It was in the trash can at the Mighty Burger where she had fed her newfound friend as the two of them discussed the details of their arrangement.

"Jean Claude," she answered, studying the grimace on Alex's face as he studied hers. It was beginning to dawn on her just how impossible the name Jean Claude sounded, especially coupled with the last name the stranger had given her: McDonald. Jean Claude McDonald just sounded wrong. Dora didn't even know this man's name.

"I mean who is he? Like what is he doing in our car?" Alex asked, growing a little more insistent. Beverly, who was having a text fight with her boyfriend, was preoccupied with her phone and let Alex do the fact finding.

"He's my friend," Dora said, smiling. Looking over her shoulder at Alex, she felt him staring at her from behind his sunglasses. She wondered how convincing she sounded. From the looks of it, she felt she must have been doing pretty well. Alex had that disgusted look on his face he got when he felt like the umpire had made a bad call. Glad Alex was wearing sunglasses; Dora knew the look in his eyes would have killed her.

"Hi," said Jean Claude. He held up his hand in a half wave as he turned to make eye contact with Alex and Beverly and flashed them a warm smile. His tone was sophisticated and eloquent, and his teeth were perfect and sparkling white—too perfect and too white for a bum, Dora observed.

"We couldn't get away from the school fast enough," Dora told Maria.

"Let's go before somebody sees him in the car with us," Alex said, putting a little extra disgust on the word *him*.

"Well, that is the response you're looking for. I just wish your whipping boyfriend was a school teacher or a guy who works at the grocery store. Then I would feel better about things, but it's done now. Just get rid of him as soon as your kids are totally grossed out, which shouldn't take long from the sound of things. Your kids are going to accept this Chip guy with open arms. He'll be a superhero compared to this loser," Maria added with confidence.

It was after midnight again before she and Maria finally said good-bye and much later before Dora felt herself getting sleepy. She lay there a long time contemplating Maria's comment about her confidence and turning into "one of those women who needs to rescue some loser." She was sure she wasn't trying to rescue Jean Claude, but her confidence was another matter. Dora took another peek outside. The lights in the apartment were still off.

Chapter 16

Home from band practice and not being too thrilled about the stranger their mom had introduced as her friend Alex and Beverly wasted no time hurrying out of the minivan that afternoon. Jean Claude looked more than a little out of place standing by its opened door. Having seen his mom and this scruffy looking man pull into the driveway Curtis suddenly lost interest in the tree he had been climbing and came over for a closer look.

"That's a cool name," Curtis said, shaking the hand of the stranger. The man wore a half-dry army coat and carried a tattered suitcase. *Starved for male attention*, Dora thought sadly as she studied the unlikely pair. Emily stood close to her, having come outside after Alex announced, "Mom's brought home a bum," before slamming his bedroom door shut.

No one saw Dani watching through the living room window.

"Mommy, he looks scary," Emily said, looking up at her mom. Her eyes were giant question marks. Dora watched her daughter studying the grungy-looking bearded man in raggedy clothes.

Leaving her mom, Emily, Curtis, and this Jean Claude fellow to themselves, Beverly went in the house. She was upset, but Dora heard no door slam or loud exclamation from her. She quietly lugged her French horn across the yard and up the steps of the porch. Beverly's shoulders were slumping from more than practice. She and her boyfriend were off again.

"I like your name too," Jean Claude said. "Curtis is a very strong name, and it suits you. It means courteous and polite; it's old French."

"Your name sounds French too," Curtis said, beaming up at his newfound friend. Dora wanted to laugh when she heard Curtis ask him if he knew any martial arts. She had wondered the same thing. Jean Claude admitted that he knew a little but not too much.

"I'm signing up for karate when school starts," Curtis said with a serious grin. Emily chimed in that she was taking karate too, just as the idea of pizza for supper flashed through Dora's mind. Pizza always smoothed things over, but Dora had a feeling it was going to take more than pizza this time. She was right.

"Are you sure about this?" Jean Claude asked as he and Dora took a seat in the community gazebo. Gizmo had led them there after giving Jean Claude the sniff test. He seemed to like Jean Claude, which Dora took as a good sign. The night air was surprisingly cool for August as the two of them sat in what was left of the evening sun. "I mean your kids, especially the older ones, aren't taking this too well."

Jean Claude was right; there was still nearly a whole pizza left on the kitchen table. Her two chowhounds claimed they weren't hungry. Dora knew better as she shrugged her shoulders in a "suit yourself" sort of way, watching them drift quietly upstairs. Emily and Curtis, however, had talked up a storm during supper, hardly letting Jean Claude get a word in edgewise. Dani had finally shown up at the table but didn't have much to say. She nervously nibbled her slice of pizza and sipped the grape drink she had mixed up earlier in the afternoon.

"They'll be all right," Dora said, but she was beginning to wonder. She found a little peace of mind in Jean Claude's concern.

"Tell me if it gets too complicated, and I'll move on," said Jean Claude said, who seemed to be studying his boots, which had been worn out long ago.

Dora said she would, trying to muster a reassuring smile as she patted his hand, which was curved around the edge up the bench beside her. Jean Claude seemed to freeze just a little at her touch. Dora realized she wasn't the only one with boundaries.

Walking back home with Gizmo out front, Dora fended off a half-dozen text messages from Yvonne and sent Chip a smile in response to him telling her how much he had enjoyed lunch with her the day before. Then out of nowhere came Jeff's text: "EITHER ANSWER OR I'M COMING OVER!"

By the time she got to the house, Dora had decided how to deal with Jeff. In a message she tagged with "RSVP," she invited him over to "help cut the grass." Dora really wasn't surprised that there was no response and that he didn't come over. She wondered which of the children had called their dad with the 411 update on Jean Claude but decided it really didn't matter. She couldn't blame them.

Curtis joined her as she showed Jean Claude the apartment that, although cramped, was no doubt a giant step up from where he had been staying.

"One question," Dora said as she switched on the apartment's living room lamp and thought that the place needed airing out. There was a hint of her grandmother's lilac after-bath lotion mingled with the smell a house gets when it's been closed up too long.

"Yes?" said Jean Claude. He gazed about the apartment still holding his suitcase and looking out of place.

"You don't smoke, do you?" Dora asked, reading his body language.

Feigning a smoker's cough, he smiled and told her he didn't. It was the first time she had seen him really smile. "I hate those things, allergic to smoke," he added as he continued to look around before finally setting his beat-up suitcase on the floor. Curtis, with a flashlight in hand, came from under the kitchen sink where he had turned on the water to the faucet.

"Tastes good," Curtis said, after taking a big drink from the glass he filled. He walked off to inspect the apartment's bathroom. His mom had him checking everything out for her.

"Well, this is it," Dora said before pointing out the window unit in case the apartment got stuffy.

All done showing him his new home, Dora and Curtis left Jean Claude alone in the apartment with a couple of slices of pizza and a stack of Grandma Mabel's old lady magazines she had forgotten when she moved to Florida.

"He seems nice," Curtis said, taking his mom's hand. Dora was surprised. That was before she called Maria.

Chapter 17

The house was quiet as Dora got ready for work the next morning. Summer mornings were always quiet; everyone but Dora slept until noon. Most of the pizza she had left in the fridge was gone, which gave Dora a satisfied feeling that her two-legged mice hadn't gone to bed hungry. She packed herself a slice of the leftover pizza for lunch and jotted down a list of chores. Finishing off the list with a smiley face, she wrote "Love, Mom" under it. Dora left the note on the counter beneath an old saltshaker that looked like an Italian chef, complete with handlebar mustache.

By lunchtime Dora had received two e-mails and a voice mail from Jeff's attorneys' secretary. She deleted all three messages unread and erased the voice mails without listening to them. She already knew what they were about: control. That was another road she had been down before and wasn't going again. She actually had expected more noise out of Jeff and was pretty sure it would come in time.

Emily answered the phone when Dora called home to check in, giving her mom a rundown of what was happening. Beverly and Alex were still in silent mode, Dani was busy with laundry, and Curtis was vacuuming the living room. "Good," she replied before asking about Jean Claude.

"Oh, he's trimming hedges. He was mowing, but Alex is doing that now," Emily said, painting her mom a picture of how hard everyone was working. "Jean Claude trims hedges real good," Emily commented. Dora wondered what she meant by "real good" and was afraid to ask as she pictured her shrubs scalped.

She would see Jean Claude's handiwork soon enough, she decided, looking at the clock. On Thursdays she got off at three, and after a quick trip to the gym with Yvonne and a visit to the tanning salon, she would be heading home. She wondered what Yvonne was going to say when she told her about Jean Claude.

Dora finally finished up her talk with Emily and got Curtis on the phone, telling him to lay out a tray of frozen lasagna. She wanted to make sure her army had enough to eat, especially now that there was another hungry person at her table. For some reason, as she hung up the phone and returned to work, Dora remembered the tattered cardboard sign Jean Claude had been holding by the road when she first saw him.

"So when am I going to get to meet this Mr. Bojangles?" Yvonne asked as the two of them crossed the fitness center parking lot. Yvonne had been ten minutes late as usual. She had been showing a property across town and claimed she couldn't get away. Most likely it had been the buyer who couldn't get away. Dora smiled to herself, starting to regret having mentioned Jean Claude. Yvonne would find out sooner or later anyway, Dora decided and let herself off the hook.

"Maybe this weekend," Dora said. "We're taking this thing kind of slow."

"Doesn't sound slow to me," Yvonne said. "You already have him moved in, you're feeding him, and you have him doing chores."

"It's not exactly like that," Dora said, almost wanting to explain but knowing better. No one else needed to know about her scheme and especially not Yvonne.

"And what about Chip?" Yvonne asked, suddenly remembering the man Dora had been doting on for weeks.

"We're still talking, but it's just not there," Dora said, feeling her nose grow.

"Not there?" Yvonne asked.

Dora said that Chip just lived too far away. She explained that she really wanted somebody nearby whom she could see every day, and that wasn't possible for her and Chip. Studying her friend's puzzled look, Dora assured Yvonne that she was still in touch with Chip as a friend and hadn't burned any bridges with him.

"Just in case things don't work out," Yvonne explained. She knew all about things not working out. "And you might want to get to know my friend Harold's friend," Yvonne added as they climbed on the stationary bicycles after walking a few laps around the track.

"The mailman?" Dora asked to humor Yvonne.

"Not just a mailman but a retired postmaster," Yvonne replied, getting a little winded as the two of them pedaled their bikes. Winded or not, she gave Dora a play-by-play of the weekend and the fun she had missed out on by not taking Harold up on his invitation.

Forty-five minutes later, the two of them parted ways, wet as fish from their workouts. Yvonne was on her way to Harold's pool and Dora to the tanning salon.

"I'll drop by Saturday," Yvonne informed Dora. "Have this Jean Claude ready for me," she said with a laugh as she adjusted her floppy hat. "By the way, what kind of work does he do?"

Dora, not knowing how to answer that, told her that Jean Claude was between jobs.

Yvonne laughed and said, "Aren't we all." She blew Dora a kiss and cranked up her radio as she pulled out of the parking lot, convertible top down, her hat flopping in the wind.

"Aren't we all," Dora said. *For Yvonne being so flighty sometimes, she says some pretty smart things,*

Dora thought as she began to dread crawling into the scorching tanning bed.

Not sure that Beverly would take the initiative to put the lasagna in the oven, Dora called her on the way to the tanning salon. With the lasagna out of the way, all that would be left for Dora to do when she got home would be shredding some lettuce, dicing a few tomatoes, and mixing a little ketchup with mayonnaise for some quick salad dressing.

Checking out her tan line in the mirror, Dora could see that her fitness plan was starting to work. When they had lunch together on Tuesday, Chip had commented on Dora's tan and asked if she belonged to a gym.

When she told him she did, Chip said he could tell. Not too bad, Dora said, as she slipped back into her workout pants. They didn't fit quite as snugly as when she first put them on a few months back.

"Grrrrrr," Dora teased herself as she pawed the mirror. "You cougar, you." She had found out that Chip was six years younger than her. Maybe she would share that little tidbit with Yvonne one day. For now though, as far as anyone was concerned, the only man in her life was Jean Claude. Still dripping with sweat, Dora sipped her strawberry-mango shake, which she hoped would cool her off. With all of Minnie's windows open as she rolled toward home, Dora wondered if Jean Claude knew anything about minivan air conditioners.

Chapter 18

Dora tooted the horn of her minivan and waved as she passed by Elmira who waved back as best she could. She had a garden hose in one hand and a martini in the other. Elmira's dark shades were bigger than the bikini she was wearing as she pranced around the yard watering her flowers. "Getting a little sun" was how Elmira explained her exhibitionist tendencies when folks in the neighborhood complained. The only thing about Elmira getting a little sun was that usually the sun had long since dropped behind the trees by the time she made her appearance.

Finally home and starting to cool off, Dora looked over her yard. There had definitely been some work done. Not only was the grass cut, it also had been raked and bagged. The lawn bags were sitting by the curb along with part of an old swing set and the fossils of a forgotten trampoline. Several other items, which had been swallowed up by the undergrowth and hedges over the past few years, were also on the curb for the city to pick up.

In the house, which was as quiet as a church, she could smell the lasagna, almost done. Wondering why such a hush had fallen over the house, she hurried upstairs, got out of her workout clothes and into the shower, and went back down to wrap up supper.

"Come and get it," she said, looking out the back door and up the stairs as she whipped up her salad dressing. She heard the footsteps of her troupe one by one as they descended the stairs from their rooms. Still sulking and giving her the silent treatment she was expecting, Beverly and Alex asked how her day had been. Dora was surprised. Curtis and Emily followed with tired looks on their faces, both of them adorned with mosquito bites from head to toe. Dani was last and had the least to say as she plopped down in the chair by the window, the chair that used to be her dad's.

"Where's Jean Claude?" Dora asked. She was answered by five shrugs and a pair of rolling eyes.

"Go knock on his door and tell him supper's ready," Dora told Alex as he was about to dip into the lasagna.

Alex rolled his eyes a second time and asked if he had to, volunteering Curtis for the mission. Curtis was halfway out of the seat when Dora got stern with Alex. "Yes, you have to," she said. The kids could see that it was going to be a not-so-fun supper, even if it was lasagna, their second-favorite dish.

Alex was almost out of the kitchen when there was a knock at the back door and Jean Claude poked his head in. "Did someone say supper?" he asked with a hungry look.

He looked different, and later Dora would tell him so when the two of them went for a walk to the neighborhood gazebo. He had borrowed a pair of scissors Grandma Mabel had left behind in the medicine cabinet and trimmed his beard, which, he said jokingly, was beginning to look like the triple canopy along the Amazon. "Actually I hate this beard, and as soon as I can get a razor and some shaving cream, it's coming off," he revealed. Dora wondered what he would look like clean-shaven.

"Come on in, it's suppertime. I hope you like lasagna," Dora said.

"Oh lasagna, my favorite," Jean Claude said as the platter of food finally got to him.

"You said pizza is your favorite, Jean Claude," Curtis said, reminding the man of what he said the night before when he reached into the pizza box.

"Sure did," Jean Claude said, licking his lips, "and tomorrow night if your mom has fried chicken, that will be my favorite too."

"Mom doesn't fry chicken," Emily informed Jean Claude. "Too much grease, bad for your cholesterol."

"And besides, tomorrow is burger feast night," Curtis chirped through a mouthful of lasagna.

Most Fridays, when the kids weren't at their dad's, Dora would swing by the Mighty Burger and bring home a bag full of dollar burgers for what she called a burger feast. It was cheaper than a full-on cookout and twice as enjoyable—char-grilled burgers without the char-grilled mess.

"Salad's on the bar, and I made some dressing," Dora said, noticing that everyone's plates were full of lasagna.

"Mom, that's not real salad dressing; it's only ketchup and mayonnaise," Dani said as she twisted around in her chair, purposely avoiding eye contact with everyone at the table. It was hard to tell where she was going with her comment, but Dora listened for the point she was trying to make. Then she noticed Jean Claude get a strange, quiet look on his face.

"Jean Claude, is everything good?" Dora asked.

"Just remembered something, that's all," he answered as his expression returned. "This lasagna is tasty, and I'll have some of that salad if you don't mind."

Passing him the bowl of lettuce topped with diced tomatoes and some almost out-of-date cheese she found in the bottom of the refrigerator, Dora was glad to see that the quiet, sad gaze had left Jean Claude's face. It hadn't been the first time she noticed his face become forlorn.

"Alex, you wash; Dani, you dry; Beverly, you put away the leftovers; Curtis, you sweep the floor; and Emily, your job is the same as always," Dora said as supper came to an end.

"I know, Mom, wipe the counter and table down and do it before Curtis sweeps," Emily said, cutting in on her mom's instructions. Dora gave Emily a quick kiss on the top of her head, and picking up her glass of sweet iced tea, she headed for the front porch swing. Not knowing what to do, Jean Claude waited and watched until finally Dora sensed he was looking lost and told him to grab his tea and join her on the porch.

It had been a long time since they all had sat down for supper together. They used to love the kitchen. Now it seemed everyone avoided it, especially Beverly and Alex and sometimes Dani.

Chapter 19

"Not bad," Yvonne said, putting her stamp of approval on Jean Claude. While she was visiting Dora, he spent most of his time on the roof of Dora's house cleaning and repairing the gutters. It was Saturday morning, and Yvonne had stopped by between her nail and hair appointments and showing a couple some properties near the golf course. Driving Harold's Jaguar, Yvonne had caught Dora by surprise when she wheeled up in the driveway.

"Baby, you missed a spot," Dora said to Jean Claude. She had already warned him about her friend. "Everyone but Yvonne will buy into our little charade," she said. "She will be a hard sell." Dora watched the twinkle in Yvonne's eyes when Jean Claude responded with a few "honeys" and "darlings." It was actually big fun for Dora, who for once felt like she was on the inside of things instead of the outside.

"Nice car," Dora remarked as Yvonne was leaving.

"Yes, Harold's friend has one almost like it, but his is hot pink," Yvonne replied with a suspicious gleam in her eye as she looked around for Jean Claude's car.

Dora explained that Jean Claude was environmentally sensitive and didn't believe a family should have more than one car. Yvonne got a sheepish look and asked Dora if he was a full-on tree hugger.

"No. He just has no need of a car," Dora explained.

"I wish I didn't," Yvonne said.

That somewhat surprised Dora, who watched Yvonne back out of the driveway narrowly missing her mailbox and the neighbor's mailbox. She watched Yvonne disappear up the street. Slowing down as she passed by Elmira's, Dora heard her tell Elmira to put some clothes on. Then Dora heard them both laugh before Yvonne vanished around the corner. Yvonne's guardian angel was working overtime, that was for sure.

"Thank you, Jean Claude," Dora said, sipping her coffee while watching him work.

"For what?" he asked, never looking up.

"For playing along with this little charade and for helping get my house in shape and for not being an ax murderer," Dora said, attempting a little humor.

"Who says I'm not?" Jean Claude replied, feigning a sinister grin before adding, "baby."

They both laughed as he moved farther down the roof to where Dora had moved the ladder. So far Jean Claude had encountered only soggy leaves in the gutters and no water damage. They were both glad.

"You really must like this guy," Jean Claude remarked, taking a break.

"Yes," Dora said pensively, not wanting to gush all over a complete stranger.

"I could tell when you mentioned him to me the first time. Your face lit up and your eyes twinkled," Jean Claude said.

Dora blushed, looking down at her feet. "I'm just trying to get back out there again, and he's a nice guy and seems to like me." Dora thought of the conversation she'd had with Chip the night before.

Jean Claude nodded and moved a little farther along the roof. Dora followed silently.

Finally after the silence had almost lasted too long, Jean Claude told her everything would work out. "It always does," he said, the way people do when they are trying to convince themselves. Dora, with her hand shielding her eyes from the early morning sun as she looked up at Jean Claude, couldn't see his smile. In the cool Saturday morning air, while the rest of her world was still fast asleep, Dora agreed.

Chapter 20

"We've got to stop meeting like this," Chip said, grinning as Dora walked out of the Surf City sunshine and off the hot sand into the cool shade of the palm trees. Chip sat on the wooden deck waiting for her.

It was the same thing Jean Claude had said to her earlier that morning when she and Gizmo found him at the community gazebo. She and Gizmo had been taking their morning walk. Dora wasn't quite sure what Jean Claude was doing at the gazebo.

"Yeah, I know. People are going to start talking," she said as she took her seat on the gazebo bench. Jean Claude laughed. The gazebo, built by a few retired carpenters who lived in Dora's neighborhood, was a happening place for a few years, but lately it had become lonely and forgotten. Dora rarely saw anyone visiting it other than she and Gizmo.

"This is a good thinking place," Jean Claude said, putting away the notebook he had been writing in as she walked up.

Dora agreed with him. The old gazebo, swimming in ivy and pine straw, was where she came to clear her mind and of course let Gizmo do his thing.

"Emily claims Gizmo belongs to her but leaves me with taking care of him," Dora said as they both watched the dog on the end of his leash.

"I want to apologize for Alex," she said, shifting to face Jean Claude. "I didn't find out until this afternoon that he's being mean toward you." After breakfast while they were folding laundry, Dani had told Dora what had happened when Jean Claude tried to mow the yard.

"Alex came storming down the stairs yelling that he wasn't going to let some old bum cut his grass," Dani told Dora, who listened patiently. Dani went on to tell her that Alex had snatched the mower from Jean Claude and told him to go back under the bridge where he belonged. Dora asked Dani how Jean Claude had reacted.

"Oh, he just shrugged his shoulders like 'whatever' and picked up the clippers and started in on the hedges," Dani answered. "Alex had been on the phone with Dad."

"How do you know?" Dora asked. Dani explained she had heard the two of them talking.

"He was just standing his ground; he's the man of the house now," Jean Claude told Dora. "He could have used a little more tact, but he's a teenager."

"Teenager or not, I won't allow it," Dora said and she meant it. She had been incensed after Dani told her what happened and could almost hear Jeff as he put Alex up to such meanness. Alex by nature wasn't mean.

Dani hadn't mentioned her own meanness and that she refused to unlock the laundry room off of the carport so Jean Claude could wash his clothes. She had given him a scoop of laundry detergent and told him about a washtub hanging on the backside of the garage and about Grandma Mabel's retractable clothesline. Finding a garden hose and spigot behind the garage, Jean Claude had managed to get what clothes he had as clean as he could by hand.

That afternoon though, Dora left all her drama at home. In the shade of the palm trees, Chip greeted her with a strong hug, which made the hour-long drive to the Surf City pier on a crowded highway in a minivan with no air-conditioning worth it. He smelled good, and he looked good too.

"What is it?" Dora asked, growing self-conscious under his gaze. Either he was staring because he really liked what he saw or because he didn't. With her hair in a ponytail and wearing a T-shirt and shorts over her swimsuit, Dora didn't feel all that beautiful.

"You're gorgeous," he said, looking suddenly shy.

Dora almost wanted to say the same thing to him. Even with his weekend beard he looked like he had walked right out of one of those magazines full of pretty people.

Off in the distance the band was playing a Drifters' tune Dora hadn't heard in a long time. There was even a saxophone, and it sounded really good. This would be the band's final concert of the summer, Chip had explained to her the night before, so he asked her to meet him again if she was free. He did have his daughter, but she was spending the night with a friend who lived at Chip's apartment complex. Dora's children were home, but she knew she could be home before eleven, and Jean Claude was there if anything major happened. Maybe she shouldn't have trusted Jean Claude, but for some reason she did.

"Girls' night out," she had told Curtis and Emily when they asked where she was going. Jean Claude knew otherwise. Dora had told him her plans while the two of them were at the gazebo.

"I'll be home by eleven," she told Jean Claude on her way out. Sitting on the porch steps, he was busy putting new strings on a guitar he had found in Grandma Mabel's bedroom closet.

"Sound's good," he said, barely looking up to say good-bye.

"You play?" she asked. Dora remembered the guitar. It had been Jeff's.

"A little," he answered, plucking each string as he tuned up.

Having resigned herself to only seeing Chip on weekends when they were both free, she felt reluctant when he had asked her out. At first she wasn't sure if she could manage it, and she couldn't have if Jean Claude hadn't been there. Her mothering instincts were strong, and the kids being home with no adult around after dark didn't feel right.

"A dance, a swim, and a walk on the beach," Chip had said as he described how perfect the weather was going to be. Dora couldn't resist, and she hoped it wasn't showing as she sipped the icy cold beer he brought her from the bar along with a tray of deep-fried oysters and shrimp.

Making small talk, the two of them took their time telling about their weeks. With their beers half-finished and a good portion of the "deep-fried sin" still on the plate, Chip asked Dora if she was ready to hit the waves while there was still plenty of daylight. She was. Beer was fattening, and a few more bites of deep-fried sin and she wouldn't feel so good about peeling down to her swimsuit and hitting the waves.

Making a neat pile of her shorts, T-shirt, and sandals on the beach chair Chip had brought along, Dora rubbed sunscreen on her shoulders. Chip helped her get all of the places she could not reach. His hands felt good.

She returned the favor, and not having touched a man's body in such a long time, Dora felt kind of awkward. "Missed a spot," she said, going over his back again, but she really hadn't. The wind off the ocean was blowing her hair, which she had taken out of the ponytail, and she wondered how it was going to look after she got it wet. Sometimes her hair did its own thing, and when it did, it usually wasn't pretty.

As always, the water was cold at first but seemed to warm up after the two of them had been in for a while. They tried to swim, but the tide was coming in and the waves were breaking just far enough out to make swimming more work than pleasure.

The beach was crowded, but there was plenty of sunshine, water, and sand to go around. Dora loved the beach and so did her kids. Not having her children along made her feel even more naked than she was in the skimpy one-piece suit Yvonne had talked her into buying. She promised herself that she was going to take the children to Wrightsville beach soon. They hadn't been there in a while. It was close to home, and they used to go there all the time. Then she would wear her old-fashioned one-piece suit, the one Yvonne said looked like it had once belonged to Eleanor Roosevelt.

For now though she was in her "cougar wear," as Yvonne referred to Dora's swimsuit, and swimming around in the warm ocean water with a handsome, good-smelling man whom she hoped would kiss her soon. Kiss her while they were still in the water and while her hair was still too wet to scare him off.

Kiss her he did and she kissed him back, and it was wonderful and lasted for a long time. They kissed again after they walked on the beach and listened to the band, but it was nothing like the kiss they had in the water. Both feeling a little embarrassed by letting themselves get out of control right where everyone could see, they cooled things off a little the rest of the evening.

Since they both needed to get home—Chip for his daughter and Dora for her children—they parted while the parking lot was still nearly full and the band was just getting warmed up. With the scent of the salty breeze and Chip's cologne lingering in her senses, Dora was back on Highway 17, which was becoming familiar after a third weekend in a row of trekking to Surf City. The memory of their kiss remained on her lips, and she tingled all the way home.

The house was quiet when she returned. Everyone was piled in the living room watching some old monster movie that would have Curtis and Emily in bed with her by midnight. Slipping upstairs unnoticed made Dora consider having her children's hearing tested. In a way though, she was glad they hadn't heard her. It meant fewer questions, and fewer questions meant fewer answers, and fewer answers meant fewer lies.

Slipping out of her shorts and her swimsuit, which Chip had seemed to like though it was a little too sexy for her taste, Dora jumped into the warm shower and poured on the shampoo and conditioner, lots of conditioner. *No need to look like the bride of Frankenstein*, she thought, smiling to herself as she washed away all but the memories.

"Mom's home," she heard Curtis say from her bedroom. He must have seen the minivan in the driveway. Deep into the movie, no one responded. Then she heard Dani tell Alex that his feet were stinking.

"It's your breath," Alex told Dani, and then they were all quiet again. Brotherly and sisterly love, Dora had been an only child and missed out on that.

Lying in the cool darkness of her bedroom and listening to her children downstairs, Dora felt herself drifting off to sleep to the sound of guitar music. She had heard it in the shower and wondered if someone had left a radio on, but now away from the shower she realized the music was coming from outside—from her backyard.

When the AC unit outside settled down for the night, she could make out the guitar's song. It sounded sad and sweet, and after a while she recognized it, *Moonlight Sonata*.

"Just a little," Dora said, thinking of Jean Claude's answer when she saw him stringing Jeff's old guitar and asked if he played.

He was playing the guitar in a way it had never been played before. Dora stole a peek through the miniblinds. On the top step, tucked away in the shadows, Jean Claude sat alone with the guitar. Quietly she raised the window and crawled back into bed hoping the AC unit was off for the night and wouldn't interrupt her concert. Texting a smile to Chip, she closed her eyes and let the music outside her window carry her away. It wouldn't be long before the movie downstairs was over and her rug rats would come creeping into her room and under the safety of the covers of their mama bear.

Chapter 21

Dora wasn't a mama bear the next morning when she answered the door; she was a grizzly. It took some effort, but she was able to reign in her frustration as Jeff stood staring at her through the screen door. It was a quarter to seven and he woke her, demanding his guitar. Saying nothing, Dora simply turned and left Jeff on the porch with his hands on his hips. She went through the house, out the back door, up the apartment steps, and knocked on Jean Claude's door. Jean Claude was already up and dressed, and that made her feel a little better. She was in her nightgown and robe.

After she explained to him that her ex-husband wanted his guitar, Jean Claude brought it to the door in its case and apologized for causing problems.

"No problem," she said, taking the guitar and wondering which of the children had called their dad. Jeff couldn't even play the old guitar, but that wasn't why he wanted it.

Once she handed the guitar case to Jeff, he opened it with a suspicious look, took out the guitar, and strummed it as if he really knew what he was doing. Then he inspected it for scratches.

"This wasn't here," he said, pointing to a scratch on the neck.

"Yes it was," Dora fired back in a low growl, actually glad he was checking things out. She didn't want to have to deal with his calls and whining accusations after he left.

"Maybe it was," he said, putting it back in the case and giving her a smug look of victory. Stacey was in the car. Her look was smug too. Dora waved and shot Stacey a big grin, thinking to herself, *Poor girl.*

"Good-bye," Dora said in a tone that unmistakably meant "Get your stuff and go, and don't make me tell you again."

Before Dora reached the top of the stairs, she heard a cell phone ring. The sound came from Beverly's room. Mystery solved. Too awake to go back to bed, she jostled Curtis and Emily and tickled them both as she whispered in their ears, "French toast." They loved French toast.

"Jean Claude does too, Mom, 'cause he's French," Curtis said, wiping the sleep out of his eyes. Dora remembered the look on Jean Claude's face when she had asked him for the guitar.

"Good, he can join us for breakfast and even go to church if he wants," Dora replied, heading toward the kitchen to make good on her promise. Showing up at church with Jean Claude would raise a lot of questions, but it really didn't matter. She wondered if he would accept her invitation and if Chip really was a churchgoer as he said.

Maybe so, Dora thought, getting to work on the breakfast she knew would put smiles on her children's faces. Their dad might be the king of pancakes, but he couldn't touch her French toast, and her children let everybody know it. Following an old recipe in which the main ingredient was a mother's love, Dora started cracking eggs and fired up the stove. She loved being a mother and cooking for her children. It wouldn't be long, she knew, before her little helpers showed up ready to stir and mix and dip. She loved this too, having her children with her in the kitchen. It was always a special time.

Chapter 22

Dora's minivan pulled into the crowded church parking lot only a few minutes late. This was surprising, considering how Beverly and Alex had dawdled around, especially Alex. Dora hadn't talked to him yet about his behavior toward Jean Claude. She planned to do that after church. Where all this venom was coming from she couldn't say, but she felt sure Jeff had something to do with it.

Jean Claude was riding shotgun and actually dressed better than Dora had anticipated, considering the clothes he had been wearing since she met him. He also had shaved, and she hardly recognized him when he showed up for breakfast. He had a strong jaw line and a nice profile, much too nice to be hiding behind a scruffy beard. But she had never been homeless and lived a bum's life and couldn't say for sure that wearing a beard wasn't for the best.

"He's going?" Alex asked in a whiny voice that really got under Dora's skin. He sounded like Jeff when he did that.

Dora answered yes as Alex took his seat at the kitchen table across from Jean Claude, who had almost finished off the French toast Dora had served him.

"Are you really French?" Dani asked. "Curtis says you are."

"Oui," Jean Claude said before taking another bite of French toast dripping with maple syrup. He looked surprised. It was the first time Dani had spoken to him since her mom had brought him home.

"That means yes," Beverly explained to Dani. Beverly had taken first-semester French in the spring.

Dani told her she already knew that. It was something she had learned at summer camp.

It was Beverly's turn for questions and answers, and she had some ready. "Were you born in France?" she asked.

"My mom was," Jean Claude said, a little surprised at Beverly's newfound interest in him. Seeming somewhat satisfied with Jean Claude's answer, she silently rehearsed her next question before asking.

"Do you French kiss?" Beverly finally asked with a somewhat bold hesitation.

"You're gross," said Dani.

"Yeah, we're trying to eat here," Alex added, looking even more cross.

"What's gross?" asked Emily, holding a glass of orange juice in one hand and French toast in the other and trying to figure out what French kissing was. Curtis was in his own world, and Dora was glad.

"Tongue kissing," Dani answered. She had learned about that at summer camp also.

"Enough," said Dora, cutting Beverly a razor-sharp look.

Jean Claude smiled, a little embarrassed, as he swirled his last piece of French toast through the remaining syrup on his plate. When he was sure he had gotten all of the syrup possible, he took his last bite before washing it down with some orange juice and stood up. Making his way around the kitchen table, he leaned over and kissed Dora on the cheek. All five children dropped their forks. "My compliments," Jean Claude said in a husky voice as Dora felt the sticky syrup from his lips on her cheeks. Her face felt suddenly crimson.

With everyone's eyes on their mom, they didn't see Jean Claude's wink before he went out to the porch while everyone else finished getting ready for church.

As always the getting ready seemed to take forever, but it really didn't. Arriving at the church a little late, the six of them managed to find a seat before the second hymn had started. Not too many people noticed as Dora, the children, and Jean Claude came in and took their places in the second to last pew.

Dora wanting something different after she and Jeff divorced and had visited a few churches before finding one she felt was right for her. In the sanctuary of what she now called "her church," Dora felt safe and welcomed, and her kids liked it too. Even though it was small and didn't have a lot of stained glass and intricate woodwork like the church she grew up in, this little church had a warm glow—a glow that came from the people there who had reached out to her with open arms and hugs. The little church had been good for Dora and for her children. She never missed a Sunday service.

The six if them hadn't been sitting there long when Beulah Smith looked back at Dora with a curious gaze. Dora politely returned Beulah's gaze with a smile, and so did Jean Claude, who was second to fall under her inquisitive gaze. It was obvious Beulah didn't quite know what to make of Jean Claude. She had never seen a man with Dora at church.

"Something stinks, Mom," Curtis whispered. He was right: something did stink. Dora had caught a whiff of it as she sat down. Looking around, Dora tried to figure out where the awful smell was coming from, and she wasn't the only one. The lady next to Beulah was pinching her nose and pointing behind her to where Dora, Jean Claude, and the children were seated.

"Pssss," Curtis said, pointing at Dani's shoe. "Dani stepped in dog poop, Mom."

By then Dani had figured out the smell was coming from the bottom of her shoe but looked down anyway to confirm it before she put her face in her hands with embarrassment.

Easing past Dora, Jean Claude took a seat next to Dani whose face was still in her hands. He unlaced her shoe, slipping it off of her foot, and he eased out of the sanctuary through the big wooden doors, taking the stink with him.

Dani was crying into her hands, but since the entire church was praying no one noticed, and no one noticed the stink anymore. Dora tried to remember being Dani's age and supposed that dog poop on her shoe would have made her cry too.

After a few minutes passed, Jean Claude slipped back through the big wooden doors and set Dani's shoe by her foot. By then she had stopped crying, and she slipped her foot back into her shoe. Jean Claude took his place between Curtis and Beverly. At the end of the pew, Alex had distanced himself from everyone, especially Jean Claude. He was still angry about the kiss Jean Claude had given his mom.

Before leaving the house that morning Alex had a little tantrum regarding Jean Claude.

"Just wait until Dad finds out about this," he said when he was sure Jean Claude was on the porch and wouldn't hear.

"And?" Dora said, looking deep into her son's eyes with the same "whatever" look he liked to use on her. She had learned the power of the understatement when dealing with her children. Her reaction, not being what Alex was looking for left him not able to do much more than find a place on the far end of the pew and pout.

Watching Jean Claude open his pocket-sized Bible and turn to the scripture the preacher was citing, Dora felt a little embarrassed that she hadn't brought hers. She could see it in her mind lying either on the nightstand by her bed or her dresser. She would bring it next week, she told herself, still somewhat surprised that Jean Claude carried one.

For the second week in a row, the pastor had taken his message from the book of James. Soft spoken and firm, he always left Dora with something to think about and the kids with questions. They had discussions about the sermon on their way home each Sunday. Dora wondered if Alex was taking in the message about being good to all people, the haves and the have-nots. She decided he probably wasn't as she watched him flick the ponytail of the girl sitting in front of him. Her name was Mindy, and Dora had noticed the two of them making eyes at each other during vacation Bible school. She was pretty sure Mindy was going to be Alex's first official girlfriend. She had been wondering how she was going to handle watching her firstborn fall in love. *Probably as well as he is going to handle me falling in love*, she thought as she remembered Chip's kiss from the previous day. Alex saw his mom watching him out of the corner of his eye and slid back in his seat. Mindy turned and smiled at Dora; Dora smiled back.

Church ended a little past noon as always, and Dora's children couldn't seem to get out of the sanctuary and into the minivan fast enough. Alex didn't even linger to talk to Mindy. Alex, Dani, and Beverly were all sitting in Minnie and ready to go as she and Jean Claude, along with Curtis and Emily, made their way across the parking lot. The church parking lot was a maze of moving cars, trucks, and SUVs all full of smiling people with Sunday dinner on their minds.

Dora and Jean Claude were discussing how good the sermon was as Curtis shuffled his feet though the pea gravel of the parking lot and Emily worked to get a stick of chewing gum unwrapped. Mr. Smith, the lead usher, had given her the gum for being such a pretty little girl. He gave Dora a stick of gum too, but this time, seeing Jean Claude by her side, he did so without the cost of a hug. A good hug was the usual fee he collected for a stick of gum from all the single ladies at the church. His wife had passed a few years back.

It had rained while they were in church, but now the sun was out. It was going to be a scorcher, and crossing the parking lot, Dora felt the sun already bearing down on them. With no air-conditioning, the inside of the minivan was nearly unbearable. Buckled up and sweating, everyone waited for her to get out on the open road. With the windows open, they were ready to catch some wind.

"What's for lunch?" Curtis was the first to ask, as usual.

"Boogers," Beverly said, announcing to everyone that she had seen Curtis picking his nose during prayer.

"You were," Curtis fired back, his ears turning red with embarrassment. Nobody mentioned Dani's encounter with dog poop, but they would sooner or later. Now their main concern was lunch.

"Mighty Burger," Dora said as she guided the minivan onto the busy four-lane highway.

"Cool," she heard from the back but wasn't sure who said it. Dora was still wondering if Jean Claude knew anything about minivan air conditioners. She decided against asking him, it being Sunday, and especially with him in a white shirt and tie.

Dora was walking out of Mighty Burger with a bag full of burgers and fries when she saw Jean Claude coming from the auto parts store with a bag. *He must be a mind reader,* she thought.

"Air-conditioning stuff," Jean Claude said, holding up the bag.

"Lunch stuff," she replied, holding up her bag. They both smiled.

Instead of going straight home, Dora surprised everyone by turning into the local park and finding a shady spot near a picnic table with a nice view of the lake.

"Cool, Mom, a picnic," Curtis said. Emily echoed him while Alex and Beverly groaned and whined about how hot their church clothes were. Dani was sneaking a peek at the sole of her shoe, making sure she hadn't found the same dog poop coming out of the church that she had found going in.

Dora handed out the burgers and fries, and Beverly poured the drinks. Everyone else gathered around the picnic table, everyone but Jean Claude. He was working on Minnie's air conditioner. Focused on the food, hardly anyone noticed what he was up to which didn't seem to bother him.

"What are you doing?" Dora asked, walking over to the minivan where Jean Claude had the hood raised. "It's Sunday and you are all dressed up."

"Working my magic," Jean Claude said as he fiddled around with a yellow can and some wrenches. He looked like he knew what he was doing, so Dora's only worry was that he would mess up his shirt, which surprisingly he didn't.

One of the children called Dora back to the picnic table where some kind of crisis was developing. Jean Claude, after closing the hood and putting away the bag of parts, was close behind her.

"Did you save some for me?" Jean Claude asked, knowing the answer.

"Of course we did, sweetheart," Dora replied, batting her eyelids. Handing him a burger, she topped her sweetheart comment by dangling a french fry in front of him. Tickled by Alex's expression of disgust, Jean Claude could hardly keep a straight face as he tried to catch the elusive french fry in his mouth.

"Mmm," he said, smiling at Dora and licking his lips, "sweet just like you ... and a little salty."

"And don't you forget it," she winked back at him, flicking her hair over her shoulder as she had seen Beverly do in an attempt to look sexy.

"Gross," Beverly mumbled.

Gross or not, everyone agreed that Jean Claude had worked a miracle. Minnie's air was definitely working better than ever on the way home from their little picnic. Passing by the lonely bridge where she had picked him up less than a week ago, Dora thought about what a difference some food and a safe place to stay could make in the life of a person. Then, for some strange reason, she remembered the cardboard sign Jean Claude had been holding. By now it was long gone.

Chapter 23

His guitar wasn't the only thing that Jeff Ashworth came to the house demanding. A week before school started, Dora was backing out of her driveway to go to work when Jeff parked his Land Rover in front of her house. From the surprised look on his face, Dora suspected that her being home had caught him off guard.

"Telescope," Jeff said, almost sneering, as he squared off with Dora. She didn't have to use ESP to know why he was there. She knew what this was really about as she studied him in the morning sun. He was still the same old Jeff, but his good looks that had once made her melt didn't have the same effect anymore. He looked old and tired. Trying to keep up with a twentysomething must come with price, she decided.

As the sun had been setting the past few nights, Jean Claude along with Curtis and Emily had been following a constellation in the late summer sky using Jeff's telescope. At first it had been just Jean

Claude and Curtis using some binoculars Curtis had received for Christmas a few years back. Then Curtis remembered his dad's old telescope and ventured into the sweltering shadows of the attic to round it up. Still dripping with sweat, he rumbled through the screen door off the side porch with a triumphant look and the telescope over his shoulder.

"All right!" boomed Jean Claude. The two of them scouted out a spot where they could watch the night sky. Finding a good place to stargaze wasn't easy in a yard full of trees, which cast a blanket of shade over everything.

Finally the two of them located a "good position for observation" as Jean Claude referred to a little patch of grass at the edge of the yard under the open sky. They rounded up some lawn chairs and waited for nightfall. Emily, curious and not wanting to be left out, joined them. Dora, who was talking to Chip about another weekend date, watched and listened from the porch.

Curtis amazed his mom as he pointed out and named constellations and stars that began appearing the sky. Dora was delighted with his excitement, noticing that he had a book on the solar system in one hand and a notebook in the other. Curtis had shown little interest in books and school even before his parents split. After the divorce, the little interest he did have seemed to dwindle even more. Eager to get in on the fun, Dora said good-bye to Chip and joined the stargazing.

"I don't see a dog," Emily said, growing frustrated as she searched the darkening sky for the likes of Gizmo.

Curtis explained that a constellation wasn't a real dog but a pattern that sort of looked like a dog, and he tried to draw it out with his fingers for her the way Jean Claude had done for him. When Curtis couldn't make Emily understand, Dora sensed his frustration and took Emily's finger, pointing it at the brightest star in the sky. "You see that bright star?" she asked Emily, who nodded her head. "Well, that's his eye." Dora explained to Emily that it was like the dot-to-dot drawings in her fun book.

"Oh, I see it," Emily said, her frustration leaving her voice.

As Jean Claude watched, he seemed sad for a second. No one noticed but Dora. The kids were busy, their heads upturned toward the night sky.

That had been two nights ago, and now it was Tuesday morning and Jeff stood with his hands on hips, almost tapping his foot as if he expected Dora to reach into her back pocket and pull out his telescope.

"What's this about?" she asked, almost wishing at once that she hadn't. She didn't have time for a Jeff lecture.

Too late, he had already started. Dora listened as Jeff explained how his things were still his, making it clear to her that legally the house also was still his if only in part. "And just because you move your man into your life and the lives of my children, you don't have any right to what is mine," he said. She let him roll on until he got to the line, "When are you ever going to learn?" At that point she put up her hand.

"You're right," she said.

"I know I'm right," he replied, followed by a terse and arrogant "Now how about my telescope?"

On her way to the garage where the telescope waited for another night of stargazing, she called into work. This was going to take a while she decided. Jeff, arms folded, waited by the Land Rover for his telescope and other things he had no idea Dora was gathering up for him.

By the time she had finished making trips to and from the garage and attic, there was a mountain of "Jeff things" piled by the street—Rollerblades, snowboards, water skis, a mountain bike, a couple of saws, power tools, and last but not least, a grow light.

Dora had asked Jean Claude to help her with the grow light after he peeked out of the apartment door wondering who was in the garage. She actually did need help; it was a big grow light and provided a perfect opportunity for Jeff to get a look at "her man," as he had referred to Jean Claude in his curbside tirade.

Jeff did just as she expected and nodded politely to the man he had been referring to behind his back as "a worthless piece of trash" and "a homeless vagrant"—words and phrases he had introduced into the minds and vocabulary of Alex and Beverly and possibly Dani. Jean Claude nodded back before asking Dora if there was anything else he could help her with.

"The telescope," Dora said with a tone of finality.

"The telescope?" Jean Claude asked, sounding a little confused before shrugging his shoulders. He understood.

As Dora and Jeff waited for Jean Claude to bring the telescope, Jeff inspected each item she had laid by the curb. He had called Stacey, who was on her way with the pickup.

"It's just too much for the Land Rover," he admitted. He was right. He would never get everything piled by the curb into the Land Rover.

Noticing two cats watching her through the Land Rover's rear window, Dora stood for a second watching them. "Nice cats," she added, not really intending for Jeff to hear.

"William and Kate," he replied, sharing the cat's names. He told her the cats were Stacey's. Dora figured as much. Jeff never really had been a pet person and was highly allergic to cat hair. *He must be taking allergy shots*, she thought and let the entire notion go as she looked at her watch.

"Ye old tele," Jean Claude said, feigning a Scottish brogue that sounded pretty good but didn't go far in lightening the mood of Jeff or Dora. Pressing through the tension in the air, Jean Claude described how he had polished its paraboloidial mirror and collimated the telescope's lens. "It really is quite a telescope," Jean Claude said and delicately handed it over to Jeff.

"Thanks," Jeff replied, obviously not knowing what to say.

Neither Jeff nor Dora had a clue as to what Jean Claude was talking about. All they had ever done with the old telescope was point it at the moon a few times when Jeff first got it and at the Staleys' house next door once when it looked like someone was breaking in.

From the look on Jeff's face, Dora was pretty sure he had expected Jean Claude to be a Neanderthal and instead of articulate comments had anticipated a series of unintelligible grunts. She regretfully had expected something similar when she first saw Jean Claude by the bridge a few weeks back.

"What's with the buckets?" Jeff asked as Dora made her way to the minivan checking her watch again. There was no need for her to wait with Jeff for Stacey to show up.

"Painting the house," Dora answered.

"Hope you're not using some cheap paint," Jeff commented.

Dora pulled her sunglasses over her eyes and, not wanting to be any later for work, didn't respond to Jeff's comment. Backing out of the driveway, she slowed down just long enough to let Jeff know that his child-support payment was late again, putting emphasis on *again*.

Still inspecting his toys, Jeff grew smaller and smaller in Dora's rearview mirror, and she was glad. She passed Stacey driving the pickup as she turned out of her neighborhood. Dora just shook her head thinking about the "cheap paint" comment. Jeff had made his point, and it wasn't about the paint. It was about the house and his plans to take it away from her.

Chapter 24

Chip took it as a joke when Dora mentioned that she might be looking for a new place to live and asked him what he thought about Jacksonville. Dora wasn't joking. Her situation was more serious than she wanted to admit to herself or anyone else. Having to say good-bye to the only place she had ever called home frightened her.

The measured and pencil-dated lines beside the downstairs closet marked not only the progression of her children up the growth chart but her own as well.

"See, you're taller than Mommy when she was your age," Dora had explained two years ago, providing Curtis with empirical evidence that made him feel a little better about being the shortest boy in his grade.

From the oldest tree in her yard hung the same tire swing she had played on as a kid and broken her arm, just as Beverly had when she was nine. Only now it hung from a chain instead of the rope Dora had watched her father tie to the branch all those years ago.

All of her memories good and bad were wrapped up in her house, and Dora tried not to think of losing it, but at times that was impossible. In her heart she knew Jeff was going to take the house away from her, and it wouldn't be long before he did. What scared Dora even more was that once he had the house, Jeff was going to take the children from her, at least two of them.

Dora still kicked herself for letting her emotions get the best of her during the divorce proceedings. Her "just take it and let's be done with it" mind-set had come back to bite her.

Her attorney, LaVerne Mitchell, turned out to have the backbone of a jellyfish. Jeff's attorney, Harvey Page, on the other hand had lived down to his reputation as a reptile who couldn't look a Cyclops in the eye. It wasn't until the divorce was clear and the dust from the equitable distributions had settled that Dora found out Harvey and LaVerne were first cousins and co-owned the local golf course along with a string of condos near Surf City and Myrtle Beach.

"It's a man's world," Yvonne had told her as Dora broke down while sharing the terms of the divorce decree.

Dora read and reread the part of the divorce decree stating that Jeff would continue making payments on the house for five years at which time she had the option to either buy him out or sell out. Pretty smart on his part since it was the second mortgage on the house that had paid Jeff's way through dental school. Now they were underwater in a house that had been gift priced to them by her parents; they had owed nothing on the house when Jeff decided to become a dentist.

In addition the child support would be recalculated on the five-year anniversary of the divorce agreement. Dora doubted that would change much though. Jeff had been strategic all along, and she hadn't even seen it coming.

When Yvonne asked her if she would be able to buy Jeff out, Dora pretty much told her that it would be impossible. Truthfully it was more than impossible. There had been a time when her mom and dad could have and would have helped her, but now Dora couldn't bring herself to ask them. After making the move to Florida, her parents discovered they had underestimated the cost of living. When the stock market took a downturn, they were pinched even further. Besides, her parents weren't the ones who had married Jeffrey Allen Ashworth. That had been all her doing and once done couldn't be undone.

"Do you really think he will try to take the children?" Yvonne had asked the night they sat at the kitchen table for what was supposed to be a celebration of her divorce.

"I know he will," Dora said. After being married to him for almost seventeen years, she knew Jeff.

It wasn't losing the house that really scared her. Dora knew she could find a place for her and her children to live. Maybe she wasn't a dentist, but she had a degree, skills, and experience. She knew she could make it. It was the notion of Jeff taking her children, even one of them. They were the only good that had come from her marriage. Three years into the divorce agreement, it was no laughing matter when she asked Chip about Jacksonville, but she laughed anyway. Laughing she had found felt better than crying.

She and Chip had exchanged bits and pieces of their divorce stories during their dates but not too much. His wife had decided her career meant more to her than their marriage, and Chip said he had seen it coming for a while.

"We just grew apart," he said. "I wanted a house and a family to come home to every day when I got off of work, and Jennifer wanted a career."

"Did she get what she wanted?" Dora asked, curious to hear more.

"I'm not sure. She's still just a junior partner at the law firm she went to work for right after we got married. Amber, our daughter, says her mom's always working, which is exactly what she's been doing since we met."

Dora had told Chip that Jeff had quit his job to go to dental college, and once it looked like he was going to be able to open his own practice, he had moved on, leaving behind her and their five children.

"I hate to even look at the old videotapes and photo albums," she admitted on one of their dates. "It seems like that part of my life was just a lie, a lie someone else was making up. The money just went to his head, and he had a midlife crisis or something like it."

Dora asked Chip if his company sold to dentists' offices, wondering if he knew Jeff. She was relieved when he told her no. Jeff was devious, and there was no way of knowing the trouble he could cause if he found out there was a connection between her and Chip. Jeff could cause all the problems he wanted for her and Jean Claude—that was part of the plan—but she didn't want him to mess up her chances with Chip or anyone else she found herself getting serious about. With the way she felt about Chip, Dora was beginning to hope there wouldn't be anyone else.

Chapter 25

Dora's life became suddenly busy. Her children were back in school, Alex and Beverly had band practices, and Emily had started kindergarten. Dora hardly noticed Jean Claude's painting project until he had almost wrapped it up. He worked fast and almost single-handedly painted the entire house. Curtis and Emily had helped a little, and Dani even picked up a brush a time or two, surprising everyone.

"She's taking the divorce the hardest, isn't she?" Jean Claude asked Dora one afternoon when the two of them were caught up enough to take a walk.

"Yes," Dora said, "Alex and Beverly are just angry, but Dani, she's hurt." Dora thought how withdrawn Dani had become since facing the reality that her father wasn't coming home again. "Beverly and Alex are a little more selfish like their dad, Curtis was never that close to Jeff, and Emily was really too young to remember him being around. Dani, on the other hand, was at that age when a little girl reaches out for her father, and well, the sad fact of the matter is that her father wasn't there to reach back. She's sensitive. Dani's my artist," Dora said, trying to find a bright spot in the situation that continued to break her heart.

"She showed me some of her drawings," Jean Claude mentioned. Dora was surprised. Dani rarely shared her artwork with anyone.

"Actually she left her sketchpad on the swing and I looked through it until I realized it might be private," Jean Claude explained.

"That was thoughtful," Dora said.

"Artists are sensitive," Jean Claude observed, "and I'm already on her bad side. I didn't want to make things worse."

"I am surprised she let you look at it," Dora mused.

"So am I," Jean Claude replied. "You have some really great kids."

Dora agreed. Despite a few little things that were well within the normal range for children, her kids were pretty good. "Jeff put Alex and Beverly up to the meanness toward you," Dora assured Jean Claude.

"Figures," he said with little emotion as always when there was any mention of Jeff.

"Anymore meanness I need to know about since I had my talk with the two of them?" Dora asked. The morning Jeff showed up demanding his telescope she had reached the end of her patience. She had talked to Beverly and Alex that evening, together and individually, about causing trouble for her and Jean Claude. They both had promised to cut it out.

"Just the kinds of things you want them to get out of their system on a whipping boyfriend," Jean Claude said, amused. Then sounding like one of the kids, Jean Claude asked what was for supper.

"Hungry?" Dora asked.

"Yes, getting there."

"Fish sticks and french fries," Dora answered.

"My favorite," Jean Claude said with a smile as he scraped the house paint from his fingernails. He had been smiling a little more lately.

Dora wanted to ask Jean Claude a question, one that had been on her mind for a while. Not sure if she should ask it, Dora almost let it pass by.

"Jean Claude, what's your name?" Dora managed, although it wasn't the question she really wanted to ask.

"David," he said, seeming to pause and think before answering.

Not knowing if she should ask or not, Dora had wondered too long about the picture she had seen Jean Claude holding one time when she had stopped by his apartment.

"Jean Claude, have you ever been married?" she finally asked.

"Yes," he said with a pain-filled look, still focused on his fingernails.

"What happened?" Dora said, trying not to be intrusive.

"Things just fell apart," he replied. Jean Claude seemed to turn his attention to an imaginary point in space somewhere near the oak tree that stood silent in the still September evening air.

"Just wondered," said Dora, not knowing what else to say as Gizmo pattered across the gazebo floor. He had been away for a few days visiting Elmira and Chica. Chica was Elmira's Chihuahua, and the two of them had been making puppies. Dora had picked up Gizmo from Elmira that afternoon on her way in from work. As happy as she was to have Gizmo back home, he was even happier. Gizmo had leaped into her arms as Dora walked through Elmira's front door.

"Elmira, the neighbor lady from up the street, asked me to send you her way when you finish painting the house," Dora said, changing the subject. Dora didn't tell Jean Claude all of the flattering things Elmira had said about him, thinking they might make him uncomfortable. She had to admit though that Elmira was right. Not only was Jean Claude handsome but he also knew how to paint. The new coat of paint made the old house stand out, looking better than it had since her dad had owned it. She had been a little skeptical when Jean Claude suggested sea-mist green with sea-foam white trim, thinking those colors might be too light. When he insisted, she said okay. He seemed to know what he was talking about, and the way the house turned out, Dora was sure she couldn't have picked better colors. Even Beverly had something nice to say about the new paint job.

"Makes me feel like I'm at the ocean," Beverly commented as they pulled into the driveway after band practice one evening as the sun was gently setting. It reminded Dora of the ocean too. That night she pondered Beverly's comment as she listened to the music of a guitar Jean Claude had found in a pawnshop earlier in the week. She had picked up some new strings on her way in from work, and Jean Claude disappeared after supper to put them on.

While Dora was carrying on text conversations with Yvonne and Chip, Dani slipped into her mother's dark bedroom. Kneeling by the window and resting her head on her arms, she listened to Jean Claude who sat in his familiar place on the top step of the stairs leading up to the apartment. Dora heard Dani's sigh and asked her what was wrong.

"I wish I could play like that," Dani answered.

"You can," Dora said, trying to sound convincing.

"Really, Mom," Dani said, already sounding defeated.

"Really, Dani. Get Jean Claude to teach you. You learn fast. You can already play the flute," Dora said.

"I'm last chair, Mom, and Mr. Alexander thinks I might be tone deaf," Dani replied.

"Mr. Alexander is a middle school band teacher," Dora said. She stopped short of finishing her statement regarding his qualifications to label her daughter tone deaf.

"Do you like that?" Dora asked as the two of them listened to *Für Elise*. "It's Beethoven."

With another sigh, Dani listened. Dora, having lost her place in her text conversations with Chip and Yvonne, sent them both a smile and said good night. Dani snuggled up next to Dora and soon fell asleep.

Chapter 26

Sea-mist green with sea-foam white trim was the perfect color scheme for Dora's house nestled among the live oaks and the maples, which were beginning to dress themselves for fall. If only everything else in her life was going as well as Jean Claude's home improvement projects.

As it was turning out, school just wasn't Emily's thing, and she was letting everybody know it. After easy starts for her other four, Dora was expecting the same from Emily. She was wrong. Already having had two calls from her teacher and a meeting with the principal, Dora was at a loss.

"Emily's just a little headstrong and very bright," Mrs. Carver, the principal, assured Dora. She suggested that they might need to have Emily tested and possibly let her skip first grade. "But that will have to wait until next school year; we have to finish kindergarten first."

"It's a long way until June," Dora sighed.

Feeling Dora's frustration, Mrs. Carver assured her that things would work out. "A child as bright as Emily is rare," the principal shared with Dora. The two of them stood in the breezeway watching the classrooms empty and children board their buses for home. Mrs. Carver asked about Curtis. "I've got my fingers crossed," Dora told her. "So far he hasn't had a single fight this year." Mrs. Carver was encouraging. During the past school year, he had been in her office nearly every day. He was in middle school now.

On top of the school problems with Emily, Dora found out that Jeff and Stacey had secretly visited the house one morning. While she was at work and the kids were in school, the two of them had stopped by and measured the backyard for a swimming pool.

"Didn't say a thing," Jean Claude answered when Dora asked him about the visit. "They parked out by the curb and came around back where I was painting trim on the fascia." What Jean Claude told Dora made the pit in her stomach grown. Jeff and Stacey had walked around a good hour with tape measures and a sketchpad. They had even taken pictures.

"They argued awhile over which end of the pool they were going to put the diving board and slide on," Jean Claude told Dora, "and then they left." He left out Stacey's remark about "getting rid of some these trees and letting some sunshine in." Hearing all of this was a blow for Dora, and she shared with him her fears of Jeff taking the house. The likelihood that in a little less than three years she and her children would be looking for a home was confirmed by Jeff and Stacey's visit. The whole thing had Dora almost in tears as Jean Claude listened, shaking his head.

There was something else besides the children and school and Jeff's plotting to put her out on the street that was stealing Dora's happiness. Things between her and Chip had been cooling off, and Dora wasn't taking it very well. Just when she was letting herself fall for him, she felt Chip pulling away.

"It's a man thing," Maria said after hearing Dora's update, but that didn't make Dora feel any better. She and Maria had talked again past midnight with Dora staring at her alarm clock and feeling like a fool.

Maybe Maria was right; maybe Chip just needed some space. But Dora couldn't help thinking she had scared him off. How, she wasn't sure, only that she had. It was the only explanation for his apparent sudden lack of interest in her, and it wasn't helping her get to sleep. After texting him three days in a row and getting no response—not even a smile—she began to ask herself why she ever believed he was falling for her like she was falling for him.

"Just stop that, Dora," she could hear Maria saying, but Dora couldn't. She had started to feel the way she imagined Aunt Gladys must have felt when she decided to take down her sign and close shop on romance. Dora smiled sadly, thinking about Aunt Gladys and about Maria comparing Chip to a yo-yo.

"Not just him but men in general, they work like yo-yos," Maria had explained. "They will be all over you one second, and then for no reason at all, the next second they pull away. It's not like hot and cold; that's another game. It's more like now you see me and now you don't."

Dora was silent.

"I'm serious. Give it some time; don't text him. He'll be back. He will be blowing up your phone," Maria assured her.

"Blowing up my phone." Dora shook her head; she would be happy with just a smile. There had to be some explanation for why he had kicked her to the curb. She could think of a thousand reasons that she examined and cross-examined. "Tomorrow will be a new day," she said to herself before finally falling asleep to the lonesome sound of Jean Claude's guitar.

Chapter 27

Chip did call a few days later, just as Maria had predicted. Out of the blue he asked Dora if she could get away the next Saturday. As it turned out, she could. It was Jeff's weekend. But she wasn't sure she wanted to. Over a week had passed since she had heard from him.

"I told him I would have to see," Dora answered.

"Good and see there, just like I told you, it's going to work out," Maria said as Dora filled her in on her conversation with Chip. Maria's feelings about Dora's whipping boyfriend update weren't so good.

"That guy is not a whipping boyfriend. You have turned him into your long-lost brother and handyman. It's not supposed to go this way," Maria said with a disappointed laugh. She asked Dora how affectionate she and Jean Claude had been. When Dora told her about the handful of flirtations she and Jean Claude had exchanged, Maria wasn't impressed.

"More! You've got to make it real, Dora. I think you've made a big mistake letting this guy into your life," Maria insisted. "At least you got some things done around your house that needed doing, which is okay even though that isn't the goal."

Dora had to admit that she and Jean Claude hadn't been overly convincing when it came to portraying a boyfriend-girlfriend relationship. When she asked Maria what she proposed, Dora didn't like her answer.

"He needs to go. Letting him live in Grandma Mabel's old apartment just changes the whole dynamic. Find a pizza-delivery guy," Maria suggested.

"Won't work, my kids love pizza," Dora said. She got quiet as she tried to imagine telling Jean Claude his services as a whipping boyfriend were no longer needed.

"How would he take it?" Maria asked.

Dora wasn't sure. After convincing Maria that Jean Claude was really a nice guy and not an ax murderer, Dora told her that she was pretty sure he would be okay with it. For some time Dora had sensed that Jean Claude was embracing the children. It was just happening. Jean Claude was a good person despite first appearances.

"He needs to form a beachhead for this Chip guy," Maria said, falling back to military talk, which made Dora laugh.

"You sound like he's launching an invasion," Dora answered.

"He is. Five children are a lot to throw at a mild-mannered pharmaceutical salesman, especially if three of them are teenagers. After this Jean Claude character has worn out his welcome and gotten on your children's nerves, like I have said before, Chip will be a shoo-in." Maria told Dora that things between her and her whipping boyfriend needed to be more lovey-dovey.

"They didn't even see lovey-dovey between me and Jeff," said Dora, contemplating what Maria had said.

"Exactly," Maria responded, "and from the sound of how you feel about Chip, they are going to be seeing lots of it between you and him. You better start getting them used to it."

"I guess so," Dora said, not feeling too sure anymore about the lovey-dovey between her and Chip. Maria, busy thinking about Dora's predicament, explained that Jean Claude needed to take a more active role in the children's lives.

"And by active role I don't mean teaching them how to play the guitar," Maria said, referring to the revelation that Jean Claude was giving Dani guitar lessons.

"What do you mean?" Dora asked.

"He needs to boss them around, set some boundaries for them to challenge. Can he be assertive?" Maria finally asked.

"I suppose," Dora answered. She tried to recall Jean Claude being assertive over the past month or so that she had known him. *Probably not*, she thought.

Cut short by Dora turning into her driveway and Maria getting a call from her husband, the two of them ended their phone conversation. The only thing Dora took away from it was that she and Jean Claude needed to turn up the lovey-dovey.

Pulling into the carport, Dora sat in Minnie for a few minutes pondering the best way to handle Chip's invitation. She knew that she would accept, but *when* remained to be determined. Maria was wise beyond her years, and Dora wished she didn't live so far away.

Turning her attention to supper, homework, and spending time with her kids, Dora put everything else on hold—everything except how she could be more affectionate toward Jean Claude and turn him into a *real* whipping boyfriend. She told herself she would try, but she couldn't make any promises. It was what it was.

At supper that night Dora saved the chair at the head of the table for Jean Claude. It used to be Jeff's and before that her father's, but it was going to be Jean Claude's from now on. She got some grumbles and sharp looks from Alex and Beverly who reluctantly settled into their usual places. When it looked as if they were going to pout, Dora told them to get used to it. Pouting was something else they had learned from their father.

Alex was already glaring at Jean Claude when he took his seat at the table, so watching Dora serve him an extra portion of spaghetti pushed Alex's last button.

"Holy cow, Mom, save some for us," he blurted out. What she was doing was indeed turning up the gas, Dora decided.

"There will be plenty for you," she said, dropping an extra meatball on top of Jean Claude's mountain of spaghetti. Setting the casserole dish in the center of the table, Dora let the children serve themselves, even Emily.

Curtis and Emily, their eyes big, watched as the spaghetti came their way and then the sauce and then the meatballs. Dora watched the big, beautiful eyes of her babies focused on the spaghetti and wondered when they would discover that Jean Claude had repaired the windows they had broken.

"We had sketti at school today," Emily shared with everyone.

"Spaghetti not sketti," Curtis corrected his little sister. Both agreed that their mom's spaghetti was the best. Hardly anyone else had much to say other than the typical "pass this" or "reach me some of that."

Dani, who wasn't hungry, pushed her food around her plate and watched a moth that had slipped in through the screen door dance around the light hanging over the table. When the moth disappeared, she wondered if it had fallen into the spaghetti sauce. She was about to look when the moth reappeared in the kitchen. The light was brighter there.

Chapter 28

"Golf party," Jean Claude said, pausing to give Dora's invitation some thought. Yvonne had texted her earlier inviting the two of them to a party the country club where her boyfriend lived. When Dora shared the details of Yvonne and Harold's little get-together at the country club, Jean Claude looked even more suspicious. The men would play the back nine holes of the Cedar Grove Links golf course while the ladies followed along as cheerleaders. As he was thinking, Dora could see Jean Claude fishing for excuses.

"Come on and go, and don't worry about the clubs; Yvonne has that covered," Dora assured him as they returned to the house hand in hand. Dani watched them from the porch. She was practicing chords and scales on Jean Claude's guitar.

"I haven't swung a club in years, and on top of that I don't have the right clothes. You go without me. I am sitting this one out," Jean Claude said with a sigh of finality.

Finding out that he had played golf once upon a time, Dora wouldn't accept Jean Claude's refusal and insisted that attending outings with her was part of his job description as a whipping boyfriend. When he finally agreed to join her, Dora could tell he wasn't thrilled. He definitely didn't respond well to pressure, Dora observed, quite sure that things would go just fine.

Dora now had a golf party on Friday afternoon with her whipping boyfriend and a wedding party with Chip on Saturday, which Dora was really looking forward to. She hadn't seen Chip in nearly a month.

She had forgotten her reservations about accepting Chip's invitation to his friend's wedding party. It would give her a chance to see Chip, who didn't have to work very hard to sell her on the idea. Meanwhile she decided to snuggle up with Jean Claude a little and see what kind of reactions she got from the children.

"You've got to be kidding me," Alex said as Dora eased next to Jean Claude in the big, leather easy chair that used to be his dad's. She was almost sitting on Jean Claude's lap, and even he was a little uncomfortable. Dora could tell.

Getting the response she hoped for, Dora said nothing as she watched Alex squirm with frustration. Jean Claude didn't help matters by looking over at Alex and smiling a chessy-cat grin before asking him, "What's up, Doc?" Alex said his usual nothing and turned his attention to the book he was holding. He was half studying his homework and half studying some baseball game on television that was still in its early innings. With a contented sigh, Dora wondered out loud what Emily and Curtis were up to.

"That old puzzle," Alex answered.

Jean Claude had found a jigsaw puzzle of the United States while rummaging through items in a neighbor's yard and gave it to Curtis and Emily. He promised them a weenie roast complete with s'mores if they put the puzzle together in less than two weeks. On her last check, Dora estimated that they were over halfway through with the puzzle and still had a week to go. Every day as soon as they got home from school, the two of them headed upstairs to Curtis's bedroom where the puzzle was spread out on the floor in what looked like a million pieces. *All for hot dogs*, Dora thought as she listened to the two of them taking turns being in charge.

She wondered if she and Jean Claude were the topic of conversation again tonight. Earlier in the week, standing by the door of the puzzle room, she had heard Curtis and Emily discussing them. Curtis finally assured Emily that their mom and Jean Claude were just friends. He explained to his little sister that the two of them couldn't get married because she was still married to their dad since they had the same last name. Emily didn't seem overly concerned, and Dora concluded that Curtis was mostly talking to himself about the relationship his mom was having with Jean Claude. Jean Claude was nice but still wasn't nice enough to take the place of their dad.

Chapter 29

"Stylish," Dora teased Jean Claude with an encouraging wink and handed him the keys to Minnie. She had watched as he attempted a leisurely stroll across the yard. He didn't look comfortable. Dressed for golf, Jean Claude looked very different from the raggedy man she first had seen standing by the highway. His long, bushy hair had been replaced by a buzz cut to go along with his clean shave. Dora saw the resemblance between Jean Claude and that baseball player/actor who was so good-looking. Emily had pointed that out during church a few Sundays back.

"Jean Claude looks like that guy in the baseball movie you like to watch," Emily whispered in her ear. Only Dora heard, and Emily was right.

"I don't drive," Jean Claude said, sounding a little uptight and handing the keys back to Dora.

She didn't ask any questions and got behind the wheel. In no time the two of them were on their way to Harold's house on the country club green.

Dora could sense that Jean Claude was more than a little uncomfortable and almost wished she had not insisted he join her, but if he hadn't, she probably wouldn't have gone either. She wasn't too comfortable around country club types and was glad Jean Claude was riding shotgun. She told herself that they were going to have a nice time and they would be on their way home. She was already looking forward to her date with Chip.

"Around one o'clock," Chip had said when Dora asked what time he would pick her up. With the children away, Dora wasn't nearly so nervous about having him come to her house. She was hoping to find out how Chip felt about her if the two of them got a chance to snuggle on the sofa or sit on the front porch swing. She was not going to let herself or Chip get carried away talking about their exes. That seemed to happen a lot with them when they got together.

"He's rebounding. Just be careful and don't let yourself get hurt," Maria had warned her. Lately Dora felt like she was rebounding herself though she didn't want to admit it.

On the drive home from Yvonne's party, Dora felt relieved and so did Jean Claude, who had somehow found his comfort zone by the time the men made it to the second tee. He ended up winning the little tournament.

"He's pretty good," Harold told Dora. He had changed his opinion of the awkward-looking, second-rate citizen he was expecting Jean Claude to be after hearing Yvonne's version of Dora's "kiss the frog" romance with the vagabond. Even when they shook hands Dora could see that Harold was impressed with him. It wasn't just the martinis talking when he patted Jean Claude on the back and slipped him his number so the two of them might "meet and talk stocks one of these days." It seemed that Harold had found a stock-market whiz in Jean Claude.

When she mentioned stopping by the beach for a walk on their way home, Dora could tell by Jean Claude's hesitation that he wanted to get home. It was probably the golf clothes, she decided. They definitely weren't Jean Claude's style, though he looked good in them. Of the four golfers at the party, he had looked the most natural swinging the clubs and strolling from hole to hole in the late afternoon sun. He looked like he was in his element. Dora couldn't figure it out.

As soon as they got home, Jean Claude went straight to his apartment and got out of the golfing clothes before joining Dora on the front porch.

"Is there anything you are not good at, Jean Claude?" Dora asked as they sat on porch swing eating homemade ice cream. Jean Claude had concocted it earlier in the week while he explained the principles of thermodynamics to Alex. Alex was struggling Physics.

Dora had been shocked to find the two of them sitting on the porch and Alex cranking the old churn as Jean Claude gave him a physics lesson.

"Not bad on the guns," he said with a grin as he watched Alex struggling with his pride and with the churn as it got bogged down in the ice. Alex grimaced but stayed with it, and he didn't whine, which surprised Dora. The last time he had manned the churn was at her and Jeff's wedding anniversary five years earlier. This was the first time the churn had been used since then.

Desperate for help, Alex had warmed up a little to Jean Claude as the two of them worked side by side on the porch. They were surrounded by physics books, calculators, and a notebook full of drawings and numbers.

"How'd you learn all of this stuff?" she overheard Alex ask Jean Claude through the open window where she stood watching them. With fall coming, the windows of the house were always opened. Dora liked it that way.

"Just like you will, by listening and asking good questions," Jean Claude replied.

Dora's feelings were mixed like the autumn colors of the trees. She watched as her son warmed up a little to Jean Claude and as Jean Claude drifted even further from his role as her whipping boyfriend. It wasn't his fault that he was such an incredibly nice man. As much as she hated that this whipping boyfriend scheme wasn't going as planned, Dora was relieved to see Alex revealing the better part of his nature.

"Yes, there seems to be something I am not very good at," Jean Claude said as he swirled the ice cream he and Alex had made.

"What's that?" Dora asked curiously, hoping he would reveal something about himself.

"It seems I am not very good at being a whipping boyfriend," Jean Claude answered to Dora's surprise, echoing her feelings.

He followed up Dora's silence by adding, "I don't think this whipping boyfriend thing is going the way you intended."

"Sure it is," Dora replied, sounding a little less than truthful.

"Big date tomorrow. I bet you can't wait," Jean Claude said with a twinkle in his eye.

"Yes." Dora nodded, glad that Jean Claude had changed the subject. "We're going to a wedding party."

"Sounds like fun."

"Maybe," Dora said, sounding a little less than enthused. "Lately I am not too big on weddings and marriage."

Jean Claude listened as more silence settled over the conversation. "When marriages work, they are the most beautiful things, especially when there are children," he finally said with a tone in his voice she had not heard before. It was a tone of melancholy mixed with sadness and pain.

"And when it doesn't ..." Dora started.

"It's heartbreak," Jean Claude said, finishing Dora's sentence. She watched as his eyes focused on something far off. "Do you believe in ghosts?" he asked out of nowhere.

"Ghosts," Dora replied, confused. "I suppose." She studied the haunted look on his face.

Catching himself, Jean Claude feigned a yawn announcing that it was his bedtime and he was a little sore from all the golf. He caught her off guard, and with a disarming smile, he took her hand and squeezed it while looking into her eyes.

"You're going to have a wonderful time. Enjoy your date; give love a chance," he said before turning to walk into the darkness toward the garage.

Dora, suddenly feeling alone, sat awhile longer on the porch swing before gathering the ice cream bowls and going inside, out of the night.

Chapter 30

"It was a disaster," Dora responded to Maria who texted her a little after midnight asking about her date with Chip. Dora admitted to herself that it was probably her great expectations that had made the whole affair seem worse than it actually was.

As she sat on her bed painting her nails the night before, Dora had envisioned a fun-filled day with Chip, the two of them holding hands on their way to the wedding and holding each other close during the slow dances. "Semiformal," Chip had told her when she asked him how to dress. Her blue dress with a crocheted white vest seemed to work as she looked through her closet and then hung it on the door. She chose open-toed sandals for her shoes, but after she painted her nails, she was beginning to second-guess herself. Shoes were always the hardest things for her to choose. Jeff called her the shoe queen, and it was no wonder as shoes seemed to spill out of her closet. Dora felt good as she listened to a late-night beach music show, remembering her dances with Chip—his smell, his touch, and the way he held her.

"Just a good crowd of friends," he had told her on the phone. "A little dancing, a little drinking—you know, the wedding kind of thing."

Getting up extra early, Dora met Yvonne at the fitness center. As the two of then walked the track, Yvonne, who hadn't seemed like herself in days, explained that things were going downhill with Harold.

"I'm a fool," she told Dora who just listened since she couldn't get a word in edgewise when Yvonne was on the verge of a breakup.

"It'll work out," Dora finally was able to say on their second trip around the track when Yvonne was beginning to run out of steam.

"Easy for you to say, li'l Miss Pandora," Yvonne said. "I'm almost forty with no man, no house, no family." Dora almost reminded her that only three weeks earlier she had been bragging how good it was to not be tied down to a man, a house, or a family.

They parted after going to breakfast where Dora ate a fruit salad and Yvonne, a double stack of waffles. As always, Yvonne, tangled up in her drama, never asked Dora how she was spending the rest of the day. Dora was glad. She wasn't quite sure what she would have told Yvonne.

The rest of the day was pretty regular, other than a little extra dusting, which she did while she watched the clock. Dusting was Beverly's Saturday duty, but she wasn't there. Dora couldn't have Chip visiting her in a dusty house.

Ready to go at one o'clock, Dora sat on the front porch swing, but Chip messaged her that he was running late. "Be there in a few," his message said. Around two she decided she might need to call him. He didn't answer, but that was okay since the phone went to voice mail as she saw him turning onto her street.

"Sorry I'm late," he said, seeming out of sorts as he walked across the yard to the porch.

"It's okay," Dora said, and she meant it. She was thinking how great Chip looked dressed up. He was driving his convertible, the one he had been telling her about, the one he bought after the divorce.

"Chick magnet." Maria had already guessed that Chip had a sports car during one of her late-night conversations with Dora.

"How do you know?" Dora asked her.

"Because that's what men do. He's probably using his child support money to pay for it. That's what Kevin did," Maria said. That conversation was far from Dora's mind as she waited for Chip to join her on the swing. He didn't.

Soon the two of them were in Chip's little red convertible and easing out of Dora's neighborhood. As they drove past Elmira's house, Dora noticed her standing by her mailbox. Short shorts had taken the place of her bikini as she watered her driveway.

Elmira returned Dora's smile and waved, adding a little thumbs-up, which made her look like she was hitchhiking. The thumbs-up made Dora feel a little better about things as she recalled the fortune Elmira had told her over tarot cards and the glow of the glass ball. The twinkle in Elmira's eyes was hidden by her doubly dark shades, and that was a good thing.

The texting between Maria and Dora had turned into a phone conversation. "What went wrong?" Maria asked.

"His ex was there, and I don't believe he's over her," Dora said, almost spitting out her reply in frustration.

"Did he know she was going to be there?" Maria asked. "That's kind of low-classed if he did."

"He said he didn't know, but I am pretty sure he did," Dora replied, sounding confused and hurt.

"Did he introduce the two of you?" Maria asked.

"Yes, he did. He introduced her as Jennifer and me as his friend," Dora answered. She didn't try to hide how put off she was by the turn of events, which made her feel like a complete fool.

"He's the fool," Maria fired back.

"Maybe he didn't know," Dora said, coming to Chip's defense and what felt like her own poor judgment. He did know though and Dora was sure, especially since his daughter was there with her overnight bag, ready to go home with him. Dora hadn't told Maria that part of the story, knowing that if she did, Maria would probably crawl through the phone and shake her harder than she was already shaking herself.

"You've got to be kidding," Maria said, sounding even more puzzled.

Dora described the highlights of the rest of her date with Chip, leaving out how uncomfortable Amber, Chip's daughter, made her feel. The insider information Amber shared with Dora while Chip went to the restroom during supper only made the whole thing even more awkward.

"Just so you know, he's still in love with my mom," Amber said. "He's probably in the bathroom texting her right now. He is always blowing up Mom's phone with texts. 'Pumpkin this, Pumpkin that.' She's forever showing them to me."

Dora could feel herself falling through her chair. She had gotten a few "Pumpkin" messages herself and wondered about Chip's little terms of endearment that had once made her smile. She wasn't smiling now. Dora was getting the feeling that the teenage girl sitting across the table from her was trying to be mean and nice at the same time. It all made Dora even more uncomfortable.

"Dysfunction," Maria said. "Danger, Will Robinson!" she slipped in, trying to brighten the mood.

"Yes," Dora said, agreeing with Maria. The situation was dysfunctional, but she wasn't sure she could pull away from Chip so easily. She was under his spell. Even though she knew what Maria was saying was true, Dora couldn't help but think of their kiss before he had left her on the porch and the text he sent, saying he was looking forward to seeing her again. "Just the two of us and a long weekend," he messaged her, followed by a string of smiles.

"He may be okay eventually," observed Maria, "but for now be careful." Changing topics, Maria asked Dora how things were going with her whipping boyfriend.

"He sounds like the keeper if you ask me," Maria chuckled after hearing the great time she and Jean Claude had on their date. "If he only had a job," she added, wondering out loud where he was getting money to buy guitars and golf clothes. "He's not robbing banks is he?"

"No," Dora said and laughed, "I don't think so." She had teasingly asked Jean Claude if he was a bank robber when he showed up with his new golf clothes. Telling her no, he had winked and said he was independently wealthy.

"Yeah right, and I'm the queen of Spain," Maria said with a smug chuckle. "Maybe he is hiding out from the mob. Stranger things have happened." She laughed.

"Not that either. He never talks about his past. All I know is that he was married and has a daughter. He keeps a family portrait of the three of them on the dresser by his bed." Dora had seen the picture when she stopped by a few times to visit Jean Claude, during one of their "turn up the gas" phases of their relationship. Thinking back to the portrait and Jean Claude's far-off gazes that settled over his face, Dora felt something stir in her heart.

"He's just a man with a broken heart," she sighed.

"And you, you are a woman with a broken heart," Maria reminded her.

For the first time Dora admitted what Maria said was true. "You're right," Dora sighed. "I am brokenhearted, and Jean Claude, he's brokenhearted sad." She thought about Jean Claude's ghost question.

After Maria hung up, Dora lay on her bed watching the ceiling fan turn as she mulled over all of the things they had talked about. Switching off her lamp, she wondered if Jean Claude would be going to church with her since the kids weren't home. She hoped he would.

Dora wasn't quite sure what to think when she knocked on the apartment door three times the next morning and did not get an answer. Pretty sure he wasn't going to church, she made her way back down the stairs. When Dora was halfway down the steps, the door swung open and Jean Claude stepped out on the stoop barefoot in a T-shirt and jeans he had found at the local Goodwill store. He was wiping the sleep from his eyes and holding a picture. She decided that asking him about church was pointless.

"Sorry I woke you," Dora apologized, thinking that he must have been getting some good sleep.

Jean Claude, brushing his hand through his hair, feigned a smile and assured her it was okay.

"I needed to be up anyway," he said. Dora felt pretty sure he didn't mean it.

"Just wondering about church and if you were going, but I guess not," Dora said, looking at her watch.

"I'm not feeling like church today," Jean Claude said. His tone left Dora with some questions, especially since he had seemed to be quite comfortable when he had joined her and the kids on past Sundays. Part of the act, she decided as she began to make her way down the steps.

"I see," she said, not trying to sound too let down. But she was.

"How was your date?" he finally managed as Dora got to the bottom of the stairs.

"Oh, it was okay," she said, She tried to smile at Jean Claude, who tried to smile back at her. He was very handsome, even with messy hair and wearing secondhand jeans.

Still thinking about his "not feeling like church today" comment, Dora stopped by Mighty Burger after the service and grabbed lunch for her and Jean Claude. Maybe he wasn't feeling like church, but she was pretty sure he wouldn't turn down a big, juicy burger.

He didn't, and as the two of them sat on the porch swing enjoying their lunch, Dora told him what a great sermon he had missed.

"Sounds good" was pretty much Jean Claude's reply to every part of the message Dora tried to share with him. It was as if he was trying to tune her out, and that was strange behavior for Jean Claude.

Finally Dora gave up and asked Jean Claude if he wanted to go to the beach. He had been even quieter than usual while the two of them ate. He seemed to be studying the leaves that were beginning to blanket the ground.

"The beach is lonely this time of year," he replied, "makes for a good thinking place."

Dora wasn't looking for a thinking place; she just wanted to get out of the house and find something to do besides dwell on her date with Chip Fowler. The beach with the waves crashing and a breeze blowing was perfect.

Jean Claude finally agreed that the beach might not be a bad idea as he finished off his milk shake.

Once there, the two walked aimlessly and silently. The incoming tide was beginning to nibble away at the shore, and the pier they walked toward seemed almost as far away as Dora's thoughts. Strangely, she felt herself almost reach out and take Jean Claude's hand in hers while they walked.

On the way home Dora confessed that the date with Chip hadn't gone the way she had hoped. Jean Claude just listened as she told him about Chip's ex-wife and daughter being there and how she felt before finally realizing she was doing all the talking.

"You probably don't want to hear all of this," she said apologetically.

"It's okay, Dora," Jean Claude assured her. "Sounds like you need to talk about it. Really, I don't mind." He continued to listen, occasionally turning so their eyes met.

"I just don't know if he asks me out again, if I should accept."

"Yeah, that's a hard call to make," he agreed, adding little to what Dora already knew.

"You like him, don't you," Jean Claude said as a matter of observation.

Dora didn't need to reply; they both knew. "I'm not sure," she said, which suddenly felt more true than it had before she and Jean Claude had walked along the beach. She remembered her walks with Chip and how different he had turned out to be from the man she had gotten to know early on.

"Maybe we're all just pretenders," she said.

"Maybe, but not all," Jean Claude replied. He shot her a quick glance before pointing at a beautiful old tree by the highway.

Dora had passed by the tree for years and never noticed it. Wondering what a tree had to do with anything they were talking about, she paused and gave it as much attention as she could while driving. It was a pretty tree.

"Some people are real," Jean Claude said, "and those are the best kind. But they don't come along very often. Mostly though, just like that tree we just passed, people change."

"I've never known too many real ones," Dora said, thinking over her friends, the people she worked with, and even Maria.

"Me either," added Jean Claude.

As darkness settled over them, Dora hoped she would get home before Jeff dropped off the kids. Her five showing up to an empty house and a locked door made Dora feel impatient.

It was well past their bedtime when Jeff finally got the kids home. Dora and Jean Claude were sitting on the porch swing continuing their discussion of love and people, which both admitted they knew very little about, when the kids piled out of the Land Rover. Looking beat, they dragged their overnight bags behind them as they crossed the yard. Jeff always brought them home tired.

One by one she watched them pass by. Alex stopped long enough to tell his mom that their dad might be taking them to the mountains "to visit Meemaw and Poppy for a couple of days if the hurricane comes our way." Then he disappeared into the house.

"That sounds good," Dora said, but she really didn't mean it. Dora hadn't heard anything about the hurricane Alex mentioned. Hurricane season was almost over.

Glad to have her children safely home, Dora followed them into the house listening to the familiar sound of their pattering feet overhead. Curtis and Emily were exhausted and didn't have much to say. They hadn't even waved good-bye to Jeff, who had sped away almost before the children made it to the porch steps. Maybe his speeding away had something to do with seeing Dora curl up in Jean Claude's arms as she heard the Land Rover turn into the driveway. She was pretty sure it did.

Dani and Beverly handed their mom a coffee mug from North Carolina's Outer Banks. They had been to dozens of gift shops over the past two days.

"Stacey's pregnant," Beverly said just before Dora turned out the lights in Beverly's room.

"Nice," Dora said, but that was not what she was thinking.

"We're not supposed to tell you," Beverly added sadly.

"It's okay," Dora assured her.

Sensing that Beverly wanted to talk, Dora made her way through the darkness, sat on the edge of the bed, and ran her hand through Beverly's hair. It was curly like hers.

"How can you not hate him, Mom?" Beverly asked, not able to hold back the tears.

Dora didn't answer. She promised herself she would just be a listener when her children wanted to talk. She worked hard to keep what happened to her marriage between Jeff and her.

"It hurts, Mom, watching what he did to you, and now he's off making another family." After some quiet time, Beverly added, "It's like we weren't good enough for him."

Dora had never considered that her children could feel the same way she did, second best. It hurt her and made her mad and sad at the same time.

"I guess it's really over," Beverly finally said as her tears slowed and she started to pull herself together.

Dora wiped the tears from one of the five most beautiful faces in her world. Through the deep-down sadness she felt for Beverly, Dora knew that Jeff was really the one who wasn't good enough. Nothing she could say would take away the pain Beverly was feeling as she fell asleep in a house where there was only a mom.

Dora ended up alone on the front porch. Jean Claude had disappeared, but she could hear the soft, sad sounds from his guitar as they made their way through the darkness. Chip had messaged her three times since she and Jean Claude had returned from the beach, but she hadn't felt much like replying, and since the kids had gotten home, her feelings hadn't changed.

Chapter 31

"It's a sad wind that doesn't blow somebody a little good fortune," Dora remembered her father saying over the years. Living on the coast, he always kept his eye on the weather, especially during hurricane season. The two of them had tracked many of the hurricanes that drifted up the coast. After her father moved to Florida, Dora hardly watched the weather anymore. She wondered why.

With a big blob of blue swirling on the screen behind him, the weatherman described the hurricane and its projected path, which included Dora's neighborhood. From the looks of it, the hurricane was going to be far more than a sad wind.

Jeff called and woke her a little past eleven Tuesday night asking if he could have the kids. Dora said yes. It wasn't the first time Jeff had taken advantage of a hurricane to let her know that she was "stuck" and he wasn't.

"You don't want the kids stuck in Wilmington with you in the middle of a bad storm when they could be enjoying some fresh mountain air," he said with his usual smirk. Jeff's parents had moved just across the mountains into Tennessee, and using the children's grandparents as added leverage, Jeff knew Dora couldn't say no.

"I'll have them packed and ready by nine," she said before hanging up the phone, feeling more stuck than ever.

For the most part the kids were excited about getting to go with their dad and visit their grandparents—Curtis and Emily especially, Dani a little less, and Beverly and Alex not like they used to be.

"I'm staying home with you," Beverly said when her mom woke her and told her the plan.

Dora didn't reply. That was not an option.

"But, Mom, you'll be all alone," Beverly pleaded softly.

"Jean Claude will be here," she told Beverly, but Dora wasn't sure if he would or not. After their conversation a few nights back, she was surprised Jean Claude hadn't already left.

"You understand?" he had asked her as the two of them walked back from the gazebo hand in hand.

"Yes," she said, and she did. Thinking about it as they had talked, she realized that him staying as long as he had was actually more surprising than him leaving.

"I understand," she said with mixed feelings. She was really going to miss him, but she was growing tired of the whipping boy charade the two of them had been attempting. Dora sensed he was tired of it too.

Wondering how she was going to explain Jean Claude's departure, Dora became quiet. Somehow she was pretty sure the kids had things figured out already.

The rest of their walk had been silent, and when they got to the house, Jean Claude disappeared into the October darkness. His guitar was waiting for him. He had been playing a lot lately.

Nine o'clock came and so did Jeff. Dora's children kissed their mom, and she told them she loved them as always when they lined up to leave. Jean Claude, who was sitting on the porch while the five of them and Gizmo piled into Jeff's Land Rover, waved goodbye. With the kids gone, Dora felt a little sad and joined Jean Claude on the swing. She asked him if he had ever been in a hurricane.

"Plenty," he said, studying the cloud-filled sky that was beginning to churn as the wind started to build.

Then she had asked him how long before he planned on leaving.

"I need to get south before the weather turns cold," he said, having already done some planning.

"Where will you go?" Dora asked.

"Hard to say," Jean Claude answered as if he wasn't too sure of anything except that he was leaving. "Down around the Florida Keys and probably onto the Gulf eventually."

Dora felt a stir as she realized how sad Jean Claude sounded.

"You're not planning on leaving tonight, are you?" she asked in a tone made more serious by the restlessness she sensed in Jean Claude.

"I'll stick around until this storm passes and the children get home," Jean Claude assured her. "This is not exactly the kind of weather to travel in, especially down the coast, which is most likely the route I'll be taking."

Then they were quiet.

"Did you know Beverly made me a peanut butter and jelly sandwich the other night?" Jean Claude asked Dora.

She was surprised. Dora had decided a long time ago Beverly was her one child that Jean Claude's kindness would not win over. Smiling, she could hardly imagine Beverly doing anything for anybody but herself—and definitely not for "that tramp" as she liked to refer to Jean Claude. Beverly was a lot like Jeff.

"I was helping her with her computer," Jean Claude added, which qualified Beverly's act of kindness as little less than good-heartedness.

"Of course," Dora said, still surprised by what Beverly had done.

"It's looking pretty bad," Dora finally said, breaking the silence as she studied the weather pattern on her tablet. She scooted next to Jean Claude so he could take a look. She was glad he was staying. During the last hurricane, she ended up getting stuck with Yvonne, and Yvonne was no fun without electricity. No electricity meant no air-conditioning, no curling iron, and when the batteries for her tablet were dead, no social media.

"Just hot, sweaty darkness," Dora remembered Yvonne whining as the two of them listened to the hurricane's eye pass over. Yvonne would be spending this hurricane with Harold, and Dora was glad. She was also glad to be riding out the hurricane with Jean Claude. He made her feel safe, and she had yet to hear him whine.

Jean Claude agreed that the storm looked "pretty mean" and asked her about the plywood she had in the garage. Dora had forgotten all about the plywood until he mentioned it. In her ball cap, with her ponytail pulled through the back, Dora spent the rest of the afternoon alongside Jean Claude as they boarded windows and watched the sky.

Chapter 32

The hurricane made landfall shortly after midnight with even more ferocity than the weather forecasters had predicted. It was a bad storm but left Dora's house and most of her neighborhood untouched. Just before the streetlights blinked out after flickering a time or two, Dora and Jean Claude had watched a trampoline go blowing by. It belonged to the Tucker kids, Dora's neighbors from two streets over.

"Big wind," Jean Claude commented as he and Dora sat in the dark, with flashlights in hand, listening to the howling wind. The roar of the storm seemed to go on and on, and rain pelted the house from every direction.

When she awoke the next morning, Dora hardly remembered falling asleep during the storm. She was on the couch where she and Jean Claude had spent the night. With her eyes closed she wondered where he had gone. Probably to the apartment, she figured, still smelling his cologne on the pillow next to her and not feeling too sure about what had happened between them. Worse yet she wasn't feeling too sure about what to expect next.

"Ever dance in a hurricane?" Jean Claude had asked as they pushed open the screen door and made their way to the swing, which wasn't dancing quite as high as it had been earlier when the storm was peaking.

"Can't say that I have," Dora answered as loudly as she could. Pretty sure that Jean Claude couldn't hear her over the roaring wind, she said it again. And again she was pretty sure he still hadn't heard her. Soon, with her hand in his, they were off the porch twirling and swirling in the wind and the rain.

Beneath the swaying live oaks, she felt Jean Claude's body pressed against hers. When their lips met, Dora was swept away. She did not find herself until she awoke the next morning and even then wasn't sure it was herself she had found. Their kiss had lasted hours as the two of them, shivering and drenched to the bone, made their way out of the storm, onto the porch, and into the swing.

Now the sun was peeking through the open window of the living room; a piece of plywood had slipped loose during the night. The air was still and hot as it always was after a hurricane.

As she recalled being wrapped in Jean Claude's arms as the storm passed over, Dora's world felt like a snow globe in the hands of a six-year-old. She was more confused now than she had been in a long while.

Still in the tank top and cutoffs she had slipped into after coming inside out of the storm, her hair was no longer in a ponytail. It had shaken loose in the night. Dora could only imagine what she must look like and was glad she had woken up alone.

"I probably scared him off," Dora mumbled, running her hands along the couch. She wondered how she and Jean Claude had managed to both fall asleep there. Somehow they had, and it sent a smile creeping across her face.

Still wondering where Jean Claude was, Dora felt a sudden rush of aloneness wash over her. Through the silent, still air she listened for him—for his footsteps on the porch, for the sound of his guitar. She was alone in the house, more alone than she realized.

Chapter 33

After showering and getting her hair under control, Dora peeked out of her bedroom window while she was dressing. She wondered what Jean Claude was up to. Still thinking about what had happened between them during the night, she caught herself looking through her closet for something he might like. Nothing jumped out at her, and she finally grabbed a pair of shorts that looked comfortable and threw on a T-shirt. Whatever she was feeling for Jean Claude had to take second place to comfort. The air was still and hot.

No electricity made deciding what to have for breakfast easy. She poured a bowl of cereal and milk, which was still cool even though the power had been off for most of the night. Sitting on the porch swing and eating, Dora felt like a teenager.

The neighborhood was coming to life as Dora heard the sound of a chainsaw buzzing in the distance and saw neighbors walking around their houses checking for storm damage. Among those neighbors was Elmira who was making her way down the street with Chica out front.

Smiling as she walked up to Dora's porch, Elmira looked around and asked Dora if Jean Claude could help her with a tree that had fallen across her driveway. "There's no hurry," she said. "It's not like there's anywhere I can go; the power is out all over town." She continued to make her way down the street. Chica, now an expectant mother, was leading the way in a sundress that wasn't much smaller than Elmira's.

Dora shook her head. She wasn't sure she wanted Jean Claude helping Elmira if she was going to be dressed like a lingerie model. Then she felt absolutely silly and wondered why. Giddy inside like a girl in the throes of a middle school crush, she wanted to text all her friends —even Yvonne—to let them know she could still feel fireworks with a man. What an unlikely story with a lot of explaining. Being private and still not sure about everything that happened between her and Jean Claude, Dora decided against putting her business out for everyone to see. Instead she sat in the midmorning sun and finished her cereal, which was growing soggy.

She responded to a few texts from Beverly, who let her know they were all having a great time with their grandparents, and one from Yvonne making sure she was okay. From the pictures Beverly sent, Dora was sure her children were much happier with Jeff than if they had been stuck with her and no air or electricity. Dora wondered how Yvonne was holding up and finally got a call from her.

"He may not have any hair, but he has a generator," Yvonne laughed as she described the thrill of having electricity for a curling iron, especially when hardly anyone she knew had such a luxury.

Social media still sucked even with a generator, Yvonne admitted to Dora's surprise. Yvonne explained that all the fun people had dead batteries and most didn't have rich boyfriends with generators.

"I feel alone without Face friends," she said. "Now it's just me and Harold in this big house, and I have no one to talk to. Harold isn't that interesting." Yvonne was still second-guessing her relationship with him.

"His coins and stamps and the stock market are all he wants to talk about, and of course, golf," Yvonne said, whining a little. "I even bought a sexy little nightie for his birthday and he hardly noticed," she added with a sigh of sad resignation.

"I know what you mean," Dora said, but she didn't. Checking the battery on her phone, Dora figured she could always charge it in the minivan, so she let Yvonne talk until she was tired and had vented all of her frustrations with Harold. Finally, after dragging poor, boring Harold over the coals one more time, an infomercial grabbed Yvonne's attention and she had to go. The two of them said good-bye. Dora was glad.

It was nearly noon and still there was no sign of Jean Claude. Dora's curiosity was getting the best of her so she decided to take him some lunch. *Maybe he's the shy type*, she thought as she put a couple of sandwiches on a tray and headed out the kitchen door toward the garage. He sure didn't seem shy the night before, so she was pretty sure that wasn't the case. He's probably just tired, she muttered, almost wishing they were back on the couch and it was still last night—wind, rain, and all. The kids would not be home for another few days. As crazy as it was, Dora entertained the notion that the sparks that had started between her and Jean Claude might just become a full-blown fire.

Crossing the yard, Dora felt more alive than she had in a very long time; she could hardly wait to see him. She liked the scruffy look he had taken on since the weather turned, even though it meant that he planned on leaving soon. *Plans change*, she thought, remembering how alive she had felt lying in his arms on the sofa.

After knocking on the apartment door three times with no answer from the beautiful, blue-eyed, scruffy-faced man, Dora felt suddenly abandoned. What a silly idea the sandwiches were and all of the things she had been thinking. Dora made her way back down the stairs to her house. Jean Claude was probably off helping someone in the neighborhood. He was nice that way.

Chapter 34

Evening came and went with no sign of Jean Claude. Left with little choice, Dora knocked on the apartment door again. When there was no answer, she began to feel a little uncomfortable and put off and decided that if Jean Claude didn't answer the door the next morning, she would let herself in. That's just what she did.

The apartment was darker than she expected. All the shades were drawn. With her spare key still in the lock, she pushed open the door and called out for Jean Claude. Dora didn't get an answer. Flashlight in hand, she made her way to the windows and raised the blinds, letting a little early morning sunshine spill into the dark, empty apartment. The smell of Jean Claude had given way to the smell of her grandmother—the way the apartment had smelled before Jean Claude moved in. Most of his things were gone. Alone and leaning against the couch was his guitar with a note tucked under the strings. There was also the telescope Jean Claude had bought so he and Curtis could continue their search for Mars and a raggedy old book he had been carrying when she had picked him up by the highway.

Lying in the middle of her grandmother's table, the book looked lonely, along with everything else in the apartment. It was *The Prophet* by Kahlil Gibran with the front cover missing. Folded inside was a sheet of yellow legal paper, which Dora could hardly bring herself to read, but she did anyway, already knowing what it said.

> *Dora,*
> *I was crazy to ever put myself in this situation; it was all crazy. I must go. Please accept this check as a gift to help you keep your house . . .*

Folding the half-read note, she just couldn't bring herself to read it all, Dora took a seat on her grandmother's threadbare ottoman. The old ottoman was even less comfortable than she remembered as a kid and still didn't fit in with the rest of the furniture. The morning sunlight filtered through the live oaks and then the windows before settling on Dora. Not knowing what to feel, she cried. Crying was something she hadn't done in a long while, and it hurt and felt good at the same time.

Studying the check Jean Claude had mentioned in the note, Dora began to cry all over again. It was more money than she could have ever imagined. On the check's stub, along with an attorney's phone number, were a few calculations regarding gift tax liabilities and an amount underlined and circled. The circled amount was almost exactly what Dora needed to buy out Jeff's part of the house. In bold, typed letters hammered into the almost parchment stock on which the check was printed was the number $196,500.00. How Jean Claude had arrived at this figure, Dora wasn't sure. She could only remember discussing the fix she was in a handful of times with him, and now she wished she hadn't.

As grateful as she was for such a gift, it raised lot of questions. She would have to give this some serious thought before she cashed the check, and right now she didn't want to think about anything; she just wanted to cry. So she did, right there on the ottoman, until finally the aloneness of the apartment filled with nothing but memories became too much and she made her way out the door and down the steps.

Hurricanes have a way of shaking things loose, and Dora spent the rest of that afternoon picking up limbs and dragging them to the curb. Three texts from Chip showed up on her phone to which she didn't respond. Sometime between noon and sunset Dora decided to take a ride to the ocean and walk along the beach.

Except for a few other lonely looking people and a seagull or two, the beach was empty and the lemon-colored sky looked strange and far away. Having done its share of damage to the shoreline, the storm had left the colorful houses behind the dunes untouched other than blowing off a few shingles and an occasional shutter that would wash up somewhere far away. The folks farther south caught the brunt of the storm or so Dora was told by Mr. Parker, the old man who lived a few houses down and always checked on her during bad weather. As for her dad and mom and other family in Florida, the storm had passed them by altogether, and Dora was relieved.

By the time she got back to the minivan, the sun was almost gone and the night air had lost its stillness and was cool. She had left her phone in the van to charge and had missed two calls from Chip and one from Beverly. She returned the one from Beverly.

Jean Claude had been right about the beach being a good thinking place. It was deserted, stretching endlessly for as far as she could see in both directions. It was a good feeling place too. The waves still churned from the storm, crashing against the lonesome shore, both caught in an eternal dance from which neither could escape. Dora felt caught in her own dance as she had walked along the edge of the ocean.

As she was coming into town, Dora noticed most of the power on the business road had been restored. Almost stopping at the Mighty Burger, she passed it by and continued home. She wasn't hungry.

Saturday came and went, and so did Sunday. Dora kept busy, getting things back to normal. After going to church alone that morning, she spent most of the day waiting for Jeff to bring the kids home safe and sound.

She missed Jean Claude.

Chapter 35

"There is no place quite as lonely as an unhappy marriage," Dora heard somewhere. She had gotten over her marriage and felt like she had gotten over her loneliness as well. During those last few hours before the kids came dragging across the yard, tired from their adventures, Dora wasn't so sure. Sitting on the front porch swing, she read a passage from *The Prophet* that Jean Claude had marked, and she pondered each word.

And a woman spoke, saying, Tell us of Pain.

And he said:

Your pain is the breaking of the shell that encloses your understanding.

Dora wondered why it was marked and what it meant to Jean Claude. She opened his note for a second time. This time in the soft glow of the porch light she read all of it stopping at the last sentence to read it twice as chill settled over her.

Chapter 36

It was crazy, the entire thing; Jean Claude was right. Dora was sad, but she wasn't sad about what had happened between them. She was more concerned about how to break the news that Jean Claude had moved on to her children.

"Where's Jean Claude?" Beverly was the first to ask after they all got in and the house settled.

"He had to leave," Dora answered in her best matter-of-fact tone, anticipating a hundred other questions. She was glad that Beverly had asked first. Her daughter had a way of reading between the lines in situations like this. She could break the news to Emily and Curtis much better than Dora could, so Dora left them all on the front porch and went inside to dish up some ice cream. Somehow it had stayed frozen. Dora scooped what was left of Jean Claude's last batch into six bowls and brought it to the children who sat waiting on the porch looking a little confused.

When Alex asked if Jean Claude would be coming back, Dora tried to hide her sadness and said she didn't think so.

"Did you two have a fight?" Dani asked.

Dora tried to smile as she told the children that sometimes things just went a different way than you expected. How true those words were, Dora realized. She waited for the subject to change and the kids to tell her about all the fun they had with their dad and Poppy and Meemaw.

"Like you and Dad," Curtis blurted out of nowhere. "You two just grew apart."

Wondering where he had gotten his insight, Dora listened as Curtis shared what he had pieced together from parts of conversations he had overheard and things she and Jeff had told him. Dora was thinking how the mind of a child was like a patchwork quilt. They stitched together a piece here and a piece there to cover themselves when things got a little too scary and confusing. Dora wondered if adults did the same thing or just kept using the quilts they made as children.

It was after midnight when the house was quiet that Dora finally worked up the courage to find out who Jean Claude McDonald really was. Alone in bed with her tablet, she googled the name on the check.

Chapter 37

Dora not knowing what to expect when she typed in Jean Claude's real name was glad everyone was asleep as she fought the tears that gushed from her confused eyes and she felt her heart shatter. Since discovering the apartment empty and Jean Claude gone, Dora had pretty much decided it was the sparks between them that had caused him to leave. Trying to put to rest all of her unanswered questions, she finally supposed that Jean Claude had gone back to his wife and daughter—the wife and daughter Dora knew he was still in love with. Only God knows why we do what we do, Dora had decided a long time ago. We can only speculate. Maybe Jean Claude had walked away from his wife, maybe she had walked away from him, and maybe now he was on his way back.

She was so wrong.

Her search turned up a number of articles on Jean Claude, whose real name was David Burns, but it took only one to break Dora's heart. Jean Claude had been a highly decorated soldier during the Gulf War who came home to find that his wife and daughter had been tragically killed in a car accident on their way to meet him at the airport. The articles that gave the most information were over seven years old, and all the recent material focused only on the big mystery behind his disappearance. They included a lot of references to post-traumatic stress disorder (PTSD) and repeatedly used the words "troubled soul." His biographical sketch and military record were impressive. This David Burns had turned down prestigious job offers from Wall Street to join the military and was described as a family man and warrior before the tragedy. Someone even had a "Find David" page, but Dora didn't look at it.

It was the picture of Jean Claude with his wife and daughter staring at Dora from her tablet that landed her heart the crushing blow. It was the same family portrait she remembered on the dresser all those times she had passed through his apartment. It was the picture he was holding the last time she had asked him to go to church.

Laying the tablet facedown on the bed, the room grew dark. In the darkness, with Jean Claude tumbling around in her mind, Dora's memories of him smoothed themselves out. Suddenly things about him began to make more sense—in a way that left her wishing there was a rewind button on life and that she could hold him one more time. Not to keep but just to hold.

Chapter 38

After the hurricane passed and the kids came home, things around Dora's house got back to as normal as they ever were. Dani with the guitar and note of encouragement Jean Claude had left behind for her had recruited some kids from the neighborhood and formed a garage band. Emily and Curtis finished the puzzle, and Dora gave them the weenie roast with s'mores just as Jean Claude had promised. Somehow the weenie roast wasn't the same without him. Elmira joined them along with Gizmo and Chica's new puppies, making things a little better. When the leaves blanketed the yard, all orange and crimson, Alex raked and bagged them without being asked, and Beverly helped. Everyone made sure the chair Jean Claude had sat in at the supper table stayed empty, and someone was always remembering the fun times they had with him.

Dora was surprised by her children's changed attitude toward Jean Claude and wondered if she should tell them what she had found out about him. She decided not to. It seemed Jean Claude had become a hero in their eyes without all that background stuff. Besides, if who this "worthless vagrant" really was ever made it back to Jeff, he might mess things up some other way.

As for Dora, she decided that as bad as the whipping boyfriend thing had been, there was a bright side, and most likely she would not turn out like her aunt Gladys, at least not in the long run.

Elmira continued her gypsy routine and seemed a little confused when Jean Claude never showed up to help with her tree, which laid in her driveway until nearly Thanksgiving. Mr. Murdock, who had lost his wife to cancer in the spring, made his way to Elmira's house, chainsaw in hand. Elmira, still wearing short shorts along with a ski parka in the cool November air, worked her spell on good old Mr. Murdock. Dora smiled, trying to picture herself at Elmira's age.

Dora and Maria fell out of touch, which seemed to happen whenever their lives changed directions. They would get close again somewhere down the road, Dora was sure. Then the two of them would switch roles, and Dora would be mission control.

Yvonne out of nowhere showed up wearing a big, fat engagement ring from Harold. It took everyone by surprise, including Harold who didn't seem much like the marrying type.

"When is the big day?" Dora asked. Yvonne giggled as she assured her that it would be after a very long engagement—Yvonne giving her trademark wink on "very."

Dora's feelings for Chip had long since fizzled, but she still had lunch with him from time to time and pondered the idea of making him her new whipping boyfriend. She decided not to when he insisted they go dutch at the Mighty Burger.

One day, after deciding to accept Jean Claude's gift, Dora made some calls to the attorneys who had written the check and they advised her to cash it. Beyond that they said nothing. She had tried to find out a little more about David Burns, but the attorneys clammed up and took on an all-business tone, ending all hopes of learning anything else about Jean Claude.

On her way to work and back home each day, Dora still kept a hopeful eye out as she passed the bridge where she had first seen Jean Claude, all shaggy and scruffy and beautiful, holding his cardboard sign.

Chapter 39

It was the day after Thanksgiving, and Dora had the office to herself. The doctors were all out shopping with their wives, and the rest of the office staff was running late. Everything was so quiet that Dora wondered why the doctors had opened the office at all. Tradition, she supposed as she filed papers, half-watching the local morning news on the flat-screen television mounted in the lobby. She rarely noticed the television, but on days like this when the office was empty, it made pretty good company.

Caught by surprise, Dora felt as if she had been struck by lightning when a face flickered across the television screen. The face looked so familiar and yet so unfamiliar. It was Jean Claude. Her heart stopped as she hoped for another chance to make sure what she was seeing was indeed him. It was. She scrambled to find the remote, turning up the volume to hear the female reporter. She was wrapping up her story about a troubled war hero who had jumped from the Ashley Cooper Bridge in Charleston, South Carolina, on Thanksgiving night. "An apparent suicide attempt that ended on a happy note," she said.

"The man whose identity is being kept private was rescued by a local fisherman. He's safe and sound at the Charleston hospital undergoing evaluation. Now that's something to be truly thankful for," the reporter said. A scruffy picture and a military picture of Jean Claude flashed on the screen behind her as she ended the story. Then he was gone again.

Without going into detail, Dora explained that she needed to take off for the rest of the day to Mary Anne, who was the second person to show up at the office. "No, it's nothing tragic," Dora told her.

Mary Anne could tell Dora was quite upset and assured her that the doctors wouldn't mind. Not on a day like today. Dora, who already had her coat on, headed across the parking lot, tears streaming down her face and mixing with the cold November rain. Feeling numb, she wondered if she could even find her way to Charleston.

Sitting in the parking lot as her minivan warmed up, Dora reached into her coat pocket and fished out a folded piece of paper she looked at from time to time. It was a picture Emily had drawn and colored and hung on the refrigerator after Jean Claude left. When the picture started getting crowded out by new pictures of turkeys and pilgrims, Dora had quietly tucked it away. The picture was simple: a shining sun, a house that resembled theirs, and stick figures that had to be her and her children.

There was no mistaking her hair, Alex's baseball cap, Dani's guitar, Beverly's computer, Curtis's telescope, and Emily holding Gizmo. And mostly there was no mistaking the bearded figure Emily had drawn beside her mom, holding her hand, and the heart-shaped clouds that danced over their heads.

Hardly able to contain her emotions on the cold, rainy, gray morning, and with her gas tank full, Dora got onto the highway and then onto the interstate. *Now this is crazy*, she thought. As she got closer to Charleston, she really started to second-guess herself. Jean Claude probably wouldn't want to see her. He probably wouldn't want to see anybody. But she couldn't let that stop her. Maybe if she had felt that way an hour before she would have turned around, but she couldn't now.

Chapter 40

The Charleston hospital greeted Dora with the feeling all hospitals have and the far-off stares everyone seems to wear, especially the receptionists. She was surprised when the lady behind the desk, whose hair was so silver it looked blue, didn't ask her a thousand questions. Instead she pointed Dora in the direction of the hospital's arboretum where she said Mr. Burns, as she called Jean Claude, had been most of the morning. It was almost as if the woman had been expecting her, but Dora knew that wasn't the case, just wishful thinking.

In the little, glass-domed atrium nestled among leaves of green and the sounds of birds, Dora saw the outline of Jean Claude. He was alone. She made her way around the curved walk just as the sun broke through the gray clouds and showered down on everything.

Looking up from a book he was well into and with an expression she couldn't read, Jean Claude greeted her with a sad smile and eyes filled with hopeful confusion.

For a long time the two of them looked into each other's eyes, and when she could stand it no longer, Dora dropped her purse onto a nearby chair and put her hands on her hips. "What were you thinking?" she asked. All the while she was losing a battle with the hot tears that started to stream down her cheeks.

With his blue eyes wide open and still full of surprise, Jean Claude told her that he had come to the end of his road and the pain was too much. "Walking through Charleston, I started remembering my wife. Remembering how we fell in love here and how this was where we had our baby, and how I lost them both. Surrounded by ghosts and memories, I wanted only to wash away my pain."

It was hard for Dora to hear those words, and it was even harder for him to say them. She watched Jean Claude struggling through tear-filled eyes to answer her question.

"All the way up the bridge I felt myself growing more and more able to do it. All I could think of was Elizabeth and our baby girl, Sara. They were all I could see as I fell for what seemed like an eternity through the night and into the cold, dark water. All I wanted was for everything to end."

Turning his attention to something on the floor so he didn't have to look into Dora's eyes, Jean Claude sat silent for a long time. Dora held her breath, waiting to hear what was left of his answer. Silently she whispered the last sentence of his note to her, the sentence which had been so hard for her to read: "Without love we are only ghosts."

Jean Claude's answer, soft and sweet, was ripping Dora's heart into pieces and made her want to throw her arms around him and never let go. She knew that would have to wait until he was better.

Looking into her soul and letting her look into his, Jean Claude continued, "And there in the darkness of the water and the cold, waiting for death to take me, I couldn't see them any longer. All I could see was you … and I wanted to live."

About the Author

This is the author's first published novel. He resides in North Carolina.

Printed in the United States
By Bookmasters